DEBBIE HARRY SINGS IN FRENCH

DEBBIE HARRY SINGS IN FRENCH

MEAGAN BROTHERS

Henry Holt and Company

New York

Henry Holt and Company, LLC
Publishers since 1866
175 Fifth Avenue
New York, New York 10010
www.HenryHoltKids.com

Henry Holt® is a registered trademark of Henry Holt and Company, LLC.
Text copyright © 2008 by Meagan Brothers
All rights reserved.
Distributed in Canada by H. B. Fenn and Company Ltd.

Library of Congress Cataloging-in-Publication Data
Brothers, Meagan.
Debbie Harry sings in French / Meagan Brothers.—1st ed.
p.   cm.
Summary: When Johnny gets out of court-mandated rehab
and his mother sends him to live with his uncle in North Carolina,
he meets Maria, who seems to understand his fascination with the
new wave band Blondie, and he learns about his deceased
father's youthful forays into glam rock, all of which gives him
perspective on himself, his past, and his current life.
ISBN-13: 978-0-8050-8080-3 / ISBN-10: 0-8050-8080-5
[1. Identity—Fiction.   2. Sex role—Fiction.   3. Rock music—
Fiction.   4. Transvestism—Fiction.   5. Self-confidence—Fiction.
6. Schools—Fiction]   I. Title.
PZ7.B79961De 2008   [Fic]—dc22   2007027322

First Edition—2008
Book design by Laurent Linn
Printed in the United States of America on acid-free paper. ∞

1   3   5   7   9   10   8   6   4   2

For
JGB
and
JWB
and
CBGB

until around seven, so she hired Tessa to pick me up after school and hang out with me at home until she got back. Before, I had to take the bus to the YMCA after-school program, so Tessa was definitely a step up. At least she never tried to bean me with a tetherball or lock me in the snack closet. She was a senior with a cool record store crush and a Toyota Corolla with a bumper sticker that said MY OTHER CAR IS A BROOM. I was twelve.

The first thing Tessa ever did when she came to the house was dig out my mom's record collection from its place on the bottom shelf of the bookcase. She flipped through them fast, big puffs of dust rising and catching the light coming from the front window.

"Lessee . . . Beatles, Beatles, Beatles, Beach Boys, Herman's Hermits, more Beatles, Wings, *Goodnight, Vienna,* Beatles again—shame she couldn't decide on a favorite band." She gave me a smirk and kept flipping. "Strawberry Alarm Clock, the Association, Donovan—somebody's mom was a hippie."

"Yeah, I guess so." I'd seen pictures of her as a teenager, in patched-up bell-bottom jeans, with long straight hair down to her waist. Somewhere along the line, though, she transformed into my mom, a regular lady with a perm and a Cutlass Ciera.

"What about your dad?"

"He doesn't really like music."

"Doesn't like music?" Tessa sneezed and put the records back on the shelf. "Johnny, everybody likes something, even if it's Herb Alpert and the Tijuana Brass. What does he listen to in the car?"

"Talk radio."

"Wow, you're serious. That's weird."

"He's just kind of a quiet guy, I guess." My dad and I used to play together a lot when I was a little kid—he taught me how to play soccer—but as I got older, we played together less and less. He took longer and longer business trips. By the time Tessa started coming over, I barely saw him, and when I did, it was usually some strange late-night encounter. I'd be up watching *Saturday Night Live,* and he'd just be getting home. He'd fix himself a drink and sink into his recliner to watch TV with me. He'd light up a cigarette, and I'd get tense. He only smoked when he was stressed out. I'd start praying for a funny skit, like Mike Myers dressed up as Simon, the kid in the bathtub, or Chris Farley doing the "van down by the river" guy. Dad always laughed at those—if he laughed, I knew everything was okay. But sometimes he didn't, even if "Coffee Talk" or the "Chris Farley Show" came on. He'd just sit there, not laughing. Sometimes it was like he wasn't even watching the TV at all—he was staring past it, looking at the dark.

The records Tessa brought over were ones I'd never heard of. This was back in the early nineties, when Pearl Jam and Nirvana and Green Day were on the radio. Tessa didn't like any of that stuff. Her records had these obscure, blurry covers, or were just really dark. And they were almost always British.

"I can't deal with all that third-rate Ramones-rip-off crap!" she would exclaim, as if the radio had personally insulted her. We always listened to music in the afternoon while I was struggling through my Math Concepts homework and she was reading Mary Shelley. The bands she liked were the Cure, Bauhaus, Joy Division, New Order, the Sisters of Mercy, the Damned, and, her favorite, Siouxsie and the Banshees. It was weird, dark, clangy, sort of depressing music, but I liked it. I liked everything about Tessa. The clothes she wore, all black and lacy, and the way she wore black lipstick instead of red. She looked like a spider-girl. When my homework was done, we'd dance around the brown-carpeted living room. I imitated the dance she did—head down, feet shuffling, occasionally spinning—thinking she just made it up herself, not realizing until later, when I started going to Goth clubs, that it was how everybody danced to that kind of music.

At that point, I wasn't popular or unpopular in school. I was just sort of there. I had a couple of friends, but they were starting to get seriously involved in other things, like girls and sports teams. I knew Tessa was being paid to hang out with me, but, still, I felt like I had a cool, older friend—and a girl, to boot. I didn't know if I wanted Tessa to be my girlfriend or my big sister. But the days flew by, every school day just another waiting period until I got to hang out with her, go to the record store with her, dance with her in the living room to clangy British spider-music.

Then, one night, coming home from a conference in Miami, my dad fell asleep at the wheel. His car jumped the median and slammed into a tour bus full of old people. The bus driver was killed instantly, along with two of the tourists. My father's funeral was held a week after my thirteenth birthday.

First my dad's brother, my uncle Sam, came for a while to help us out, but he didn't stay very long. He had a daughter, a seven-year-old we all called Bug, even though her real name was Ruth. Uncle Sam's wife left him for the doctor who delivered Bug. A few days after the funeral, though, I over-heard Mom talking to her sister, my aunt Lorraine. My mom was lying in her bed—she'd been there since we first got word about the accident.

"I want Sam to leave," Mom told Aunt Lorraine.

"He's being a big help. He paid for the funeral." Aunt Lorraine was the sensible one. She lived in Tucson with her second husband and combined family of five kids. My dad used to call them the Brady Bunch.

"I know. But he's—he just reminds me too much of . . ." Mom started crying again. My dad and Sam were brothers, but I didn't think they looked any-thing alike. Still, he and Bug left the next day.

After a couple of weeks, Aunt Lorraine had to go back to Tucson, and my mom pretty much flipped out. Well, maybe not flipped out so much as just slowed to a halt. She kept calling in sick to work. Tessa and I would come home to find her still there in the afternoons, knocked out on sleeping pills or drinking gin and watching the soaps. We didn't play music at all, and pretty soon Tessa stopped being able to hang out, because my mom couldn't pay her. I guess my mom figured she was home anyway, so why did I need a babysitter? Tessa called a few times to check up on me, but pretty soon she stopped calling, and I didn't see her anymore.

I took the bus after school and got my homework done on the way so I could spend the afternoons doing the real work—washing the dishes, doing the laundry, scrubbing the tub. My mom lost her job and gained about seventy-five pounds. She didn't seem to see anything anymore. Like, when I'd give her my report card, she'd just sign it and not even look at the grades. She stopped looking at the mail, too, and, after our electricity got shut off, I started opening the bills and making sure they got paid on time. I figured out how to write checks and got pretty good at forging my mom's signature. But, watching the numbers in the checkbook get smaller and smaller every month, I started to worry about how long it was going to take before the electricity was shut off for good.

The insurance money that we got when my dad died and what was left of Mom's savings account were only going to last so long with her out of work. I started delivering papers, but with school and taking care of the house, I couldn't keep up. I lasted two weeks before I overslept twice in a row and got fired. It was weird to have to tell my mom she should try to get a job. She would look at me with her eyes all teary and say, "I know that, Johnny. Don't you think I know that?" I tried circling jobs I thought she'd like in the classifieds and leaving them on her nightstand, but I don't know if she couldn't get hired or if she just threw them away. We had to move to a tiny little two-bedroom house in what my mom called a "white-trash neighborhood." Neither of us liked the place, but I was just glad she'd gotten motivated enough to find us a new house. I was afraid we were going to end up living in the Cutlass Ciera.

I guess you can figure out why I started drinking. I didn't do it just to get wasted, like some kids, or to impress anyone. I kept it to myself. I was stressed, and, on top of it all, I was afraid somebody would find out how bad a shape my mom was in and send me to an orphanage or a foster home. I couldn't talk to anybody; I couldn't ask for help. But I could raid the liquor cabinet, and I was killing two birds with one stone. I was getting rid of the stuff so Mom wouldn't drink it, and I was giving myself a nice, easy buzz that helped me fall into a quiet, dreamless sleep.

A Shark in Jets Clothing

"Hey, man, check it out." This big, stocky college guy with Greek letters on his T-shirt was pointing at my friend Terry and me.

"What're you guys, a coupla vampires?" his friend asked. He was thick-necked and sunburnt, lugging two twelve-packs of Heineken out of the 7-Eleven.

"Yeah, and we're gonna suck your blood," Terry deadpanned. We were used to people calling us vampires.

"That's not all they'll suck," Sunburn said, handing one of the twelve-packs to his friend the Greek.

"Coupla queers," the Greek confirmed.

"Oh, are you fellas lookin' for a double date?" Terry batted his mascara-blackened eyelashes at them and made kissy faces.

"Whatever, dude." The Greek got in the car and revved it. Sunburn hopped in, and they peeled out of the parking lot. Their back windshield read SPRING BREAK—GO VIKINGS! in soap letters.

"Stupid frat bastards," Terry muttered. He pulled the top off his Big Gulp, and I splashed in the last of the vodka from my inside-coat-pocket flask. It was April in Florida, but we wore our overcoats regardless of the season.

"Let's go." I was getting bored. The flask was empty, and there was nobody at the 7-Eleven, anyway. Most locals—our friends, anyway—took cover when spring break rolled around. Our entire town got taken over by drunken assholes like the ones we'd just met. It wasn't as bad in Tampa as, say, Fort Lauderdale, but we got our share.

"You wanna see what Scotty's up to?" Terry asked as we got into his car.

"Sure. I don't care." I just wanted to refill the flask. Terry liked everything—booze, weed, Ecstasy, acid, mushrooms—and Scotty had it all. Me, I was strictly a booze guy. It was easier to get, cheaper, and less trouble if you got caught.

Terry and I actually met when we were kids, back at the YMCA after-school program. He was a chubby kid who sat by himself reading *Star Trek* novelizations. We ended up going to the same high school—I didn't even recognize him anymore.

"Didn't you used to go to the Y after school?" he said as he sat down next to me at lunch one day, just a few weeks into freshman year.

"Yeah." I took the headphones out of my ears and looked up at him, suspicious. He was tall, thin, and pale white. Later I would find out he used makeup to look even paler, and eyeliner. He said his look was his art project. His hair was dyed black, with two electric blue streaks in the front. His fingernails were painted black. I wondered what he wanted with me.

"You're Johnny, right?"

"Yeah."

"Terry Stafford." He shook his hair out of his eyes. I felt plain next to him. I bought my own clothes, mostly from Goodwill. I kept it simple—jeans or plain black pants, black shirts, and work boots or Chuck Taylors. I didn't care if I looked good or bad or like an art project at all. I wanted to blend in, but not with the other kids. I wanted to blend in with the shadows on the walls.

"Do you mind if I sit down?" He was holding his lunch tray.

"Go ahead."

"What're you listening to?" He pointed to my Walkman with his fork.

"*Disintegration.*"

"The Cure. Cool."

From that point on, we were friends. He didn't see me as "that weird kid whose dad killed the old people," and I didn't see him as "that weird kid whose mom is a slut." Terry's parents were divorced—his dad was a cameraman in L.A. who used to film his mom in pornographic movies. She wasn't around much—she tended bar at a local gentlemen's club—so we could hang out at his house and have the whole place to ourselves. They lived near the beach and had a pool out back that was surrounded by fat coconut palms.

Terry called himself a Goth, and he said I was

one, too, even though I didn't really know it. One of his mom's dancer friends had turned him on to music like Tessa had done for me. He worshipped Trent Reznor above all, and he was really into Marilyn Manson, even though he wouldn't always admit it, because some Goths thought Marilyn Manson was a total poser. We started eating lunch together, then hanging out after school. Drinking was another thing we had in common, and Terry's mom had a well-stocked liquor cabinet. We might've been freaks, but we were freaks united under a common banner.

"You in, Johnny?" Scotty handed me the Nintendo 64 controller. He and Terry were starting a game of *Super Mario Kart.*

"I already called Yoshi." I didn't have a car, but I always won at driving games. Scotty had graduated a couple of years before us, but everybody knew him. He lived in a trailer out past the city limits, and he had a little greenhouse in his backyard. He was everybody's supplier. If I wasn't crashing at Terry's place, I could crash at Scotty's, especially after my mom made her comeback.

. . .

That last summer, right before sophomore year started, my mom woke up. Aunt Lorraine sent her this book called *Good Grief! Learning to Live with Your Tragedy,* and she read it cover to cover at least twice. She snapped out of her moping-around-in-a-bathrobe stupor, cleaned up, got a receptionist job, and took over the household again. The first morning she got out of bed before I did, I couldn't believe it. She was standing there in the kitchen with an old lunchbox of mine as I was leaving for school.

"Johnny, here—don't forget your lunch!" She thrust the lunchbox at me. It had the Teenage Mutant Ninja Turtles on it. There was no way I was taking that thing to school.

"It's okay, Mom. I usually just eat in the cafeteria."

"I thought you hated the cafeteria. I made you a PB&J. We're out of juice boxes, though. Do you have change for the drink machine?"

"Change? Yeah, sure." I didn't know what else to say. It was true, I'd hated the cafeteria back in elementary school, but this was high school. You could get cheeseburgers or pizza or whatever you wanted. And I hadn't had a juice box in years. I didn't want to hurt her feelings, though. So I took the lunchbox, Ninja Turtles and all.

"Thanks, Mom." I looked at her. She was smiling, for the first time in a long time. She was like somebody who'd been in a time warp. Like the past few years hadn't happened at all and I was still a little kid. But that was the start of it. Her return from the Land of the Zombie Mothers. Meanwhile, I left the Ninja Turtles lunchbox on the backseat of the bus.

She didn't have anything to say about my appearance before, but now she said plenty. She started going to church again, and she thought my music was evil. And she didn't like Terry. She blamed him for my all-black wardrobe and hair, which wasn't completely wrong—he did help me dye it black. But he didn't make me grow it down to my shoulders, a yearlong work in progress, or occasionally tease it up like Robert Smith. Still, she didn't like me hanging around him.

Of course, this didn't sit well with me. What was I supposed to think? There I was, making decent grades, doing the grocery shopping, figuring out how to do taxes. If it wasn't for me learning to shop at Salvation Army and clip coupons, who knows what would've happened to us? And suddenly she wanted me to believe I was going to hell because I painted my nails black?

"Hey, man, leave it for a minute." Terry was transfixed by some news bit that came on as Scotty was hooking up the 64.

"What is it?" Scotty sat back on the floor in front of the TV. The news was about how this school in Arkansas was "recovering" after some kids showed up one day with a couple of guns and opened fire.

"Man, that's fucked up." Scotty reached for his bong and took a hit. He passed it to Terry.

"I dunno," Terry said, coughing. "I can think of a couple of people I'd like to get rid of. Chad Martin. That dumbass Steve Tilley and his half-wit girlfriend, Pam Kroger. Jessica Walter—little miss school spirit. Mr. Harbrook."

"Why don't you just round up the entire football team and cheerleading squad and bomb 'em?" Scotty giggled.

"Why not?" Terry shrugged. "If I had a piece, I totally woulda capped those cro-mags at the 7-Eleven today."

"Come on, man, that's gruesome." I grimaced.

"Yeah, well, you're a romantic, anyway." Terry smirked at me. "I think it's a good idea. A cleansing."

"This is boring. Let's play." Scotty kicked the game on and they started to play. I felt queasy. Scotty's blinds were drawn, and the thick cloud of smoke in the room didn't help it feel less stuffy. I was starting to sober up. I tried to concentrate on Yoshi, zooming around the track, far ahead of Terry and Scotty (Luigi and the Princess, respectively) but the faster I went, the dizzier I felt. I looked over at Terry. He was tapping the controller, his eyes glassy. He looked different. For a second it seemed like his face was changing in front of my eyes, and I felt nauseous. As I crossed the finish line, I lurched out of the chair.

"Where you going?" Scotty was a little paranoid sometimes.

"Just getting a breath." I closed the door quickly behind me. Outside, it was bright and warm, but the breeze blew on my face and I felt better. I stood there in the scrubby front lawn, listening to the cars hum by on the freeway in the distance.

"That's not me," I said out loud, and I felt oddly

relieved. What wasn't me? Those were my friends. But I had a weird feeling. I didn't want to be like Scotty, alone in my trailer, paranoid, in the dark, playing video games. And Terry—he wanted to be an artist. Where did all this kill-the-football-team stuff come from? This was the same guy who still had unopened Captain Picard action figures on a shelf in his room.

I felt like something had happened when I wasn't looking—as if someone had come in and rearranged the furniture while I was gone. I wondered if this was how my mom felt, looking at me fresh at age sixteen and not recognizing me from the boy she knew at twelve, before the accident. I wasn't a bad guy, though. I was still me. Wasn't I?

I'm on E

Summer came. Terry and I passed tenth grade admirably and proceeded to spend the month of June getting as drunk as possible. His mom had gone back to California for a few weeks—she didn't say why, but I suspected a return to her film roots. Whatever the reason, it meant a party at Terry's almost every night. We charged pizzas to Terry's mom's Visa and encouraged kids to bring as much booze as possible. One night, somebody rolled five kegs into the house and—well, truthfully, I don't remember what happened after that. I just remember waking up a day and a half later, asleep on a duck-shaped pool float in Terry's mom's Jacuzzi bathtub.

When Terry's mom came back, he caught hell about the Visa, and I decided to go home for a while to dry out. Mom and I ended up fighting, as usual. This time, it was because she caught me watching *Interview with the Vampire* one afternoon on HBO. It's R rated, and I was only sixteen, but I'd read the book, so who cares? In my imagination, it's ten times gorier than the movie, which was pretty lame, even if it did have good costumes. But she had to make this big deal about it.

"As long as you live in this house, you'll respect my rules and my beliefs. If I say no R-rated movies until you're eighteen, I mean it." She snapped the TV off. I rolled my eyes. "And don't you roll your eyes at me, John McKenzie! Look at yourself. Go take off that makeup and get that black stuff off your nails."

"Come on, Mom. It's just a movie. Lay off." I got up and went to my room. She followed behind me.

"Lay off? John, I don't know where you got the idea that you could speak to me that way—" I cranked the stereo. She came over and cranked it back down.

"Mom, get a grip!"

"Do you want to go to hell, Johnny? Because that's where all this is going to get you!" Her eyes were blazing.

"Hell? Gee, I thought I was already there." I kind of shook a little after the words came out of my mouth. That one was kind of ballsy, even for me. Her mouth narrowed to a thin little line.

"You think you're pretty smart with that kind of talk, huh?" She glared at me. I looked away. "Well, I know the road you're on, and I'm trying to help you get off of it. You think it's just a movie, or it's just your clothes, but I see what you're doing. You're still upset about your father, and you're acting out. Just like I was. Well, if I can get better, then so can you."

"I'm not like you, Mom." Here we go again with one of her melodramatic speeches. "And I'm not sick."

"Yes you are! And you don't even realize it! You're sick because you don't care about anything! You don't care about life!"

"Maybe I don't! Maybe life sucks! Maybe I can't wait to be dead!"

She just looked at me for the longest time. I thought she was going to cry, but she didn't. I didn't care what she did. Who was she to tell me I was sick? What did she know about anything, anyway? Sometimes I wished she'd go back to being a zombie.

"You're to stay in your room tonight." She whisked out, slamming the door behind her. I waited a minute, then grabbed my coat and jumped out the window.

"Hey, can I come in?" the sliding glass door between Terry's room and the pool was open a crack, but I didn't know if his mom was around.

"Yeah. She's not here." I pushed the door open and went inside. Terry was listening to some thrashy-sounding music I didn't recognize and smoking a foul-smelling joint.

"Who is this?" I reached under the bed and found a half-full bottle of vodka I'd stashed there during the last party.

"Korn. They're pretty good." Terry held out the joint to me.

"No thanks." I unscrewed the top and took a long swig out of the bottle. "Man, my mom just gave me hell for watching *Interview with the Vampire*."

"We already saw that movie. And it was pretty lame, anyway."

"I know! But it's rated R."

"Ooh, big wow. Fake blood, call the cops."

"Seriously." I shook my head. I wasn't really crazy about this band Korn. They were more like heavy metal or something. Terry liked that kind of stuff sometimes, though. "So what's going on tonight?"

"The Tower. I think Stephanie's gonna be there."

"Cool." Stephanie had shown up at one of Terry's parties and become his latest crush. The Tower was a five-floor dance club over in Ybor, and they had some pretty good Goth and Industrial nights. They had a good DJ on one floor who played some of the more pop stuff—Depeche Mode, Siouxsie, the Cure—which I liked better anyway. It was eighteen to dance, twenty-one to drink, like a lot of the clubs in Tampa, but we got in because the door guy was Scotty's brother.

That night the Tower was pretty packed. Terry found Stephanie and started dancing with her. I met girls there sometimes, but I never got anywhere with them. They were sweet, but they mostly wanted to dance by themselves. Tessa was there with her husband, Dave, her former record-store crush. Now they were running the place together.

"Johnny!" She gave me a big hug.

"Hey."

"Are you okay?" Tessa studied my face.

"Yeah, I just got a headache. How's it going, Dave?" Truthfully, I wasn't feeling too good. I did have a headache, but I was also drunker than usual. I'd finished off the vodka at Terry's house and then had a couple of drinks when we first got to the club. I thought they'd make the headache go away, but it was just getting worse.

I managed to make it through a conversation with Tessa and Dave, then escaped to the bathroom to splash cold water on my face. Terry followed me in.

"You look like shit," Terry remarked.

"I know." I looked in the mirror. Beneath the fluorescents, I was the color of acid-washed jeans. "My head's killing me."

"You wanna try some Ecstasy?" Terry opened his palm and showed me a little blue pill. "Stephanie gave it to me."

"No thanks." I dried my face and reapplied my eyeliner, my hand shaking. Terry gulped the pill, cupping his hands beneath the tap to wash it down.

When we finished our respective rituals, we headed back out to the dance floor.

My head wouldn't stop hurting. I wanted to leave, but Terry was dancing with Stephanie and I sure as hell wasn't going home. Not this drunk. The DJ was blasting New Order. I went to sit on one of the velvet couches in the back. I closed my eyes. The music was thumping in time with the throb in my head.

"Johnny?" I opened my eyes. It was Tessa.

"Oh. Hi."

"Are you *sure* you're okay?" She sat down next to me.

"I'm just . . . I'm a little drunk. I was just thinking . . . you know, everything changes so fast. I wanna try and get better—"

"What?" She leaned in closer. I closed my eyes again.

"Noth—nevermind."

"There you are!" Another girl was standing above me. It took me a second to realize it was Stephanie. Terry was right behind her. "Terry said you weren't feeling good. You want a Tylenol?"

"Yeah, sure."

She sat down beside me and started rummaging through her purse. She opened a tiny metal pillbox.

"Okay, here. Wait, no." She took back the pills and put them back. "I almost gave you the wrong thing." She smiled at me and consulted another pillbox. "Here, these are the right ones." She put two little white pills in my hand. She gave me her drink and I washed them down. Amaretto sour.

I closed my eyes again. They were all talking, but their voices melted together into an up-and-down hum. Off in the distance, the DJ put on a song I recognized. "Never Enough," by the Cure. Stephanie and Terry left to dance. I opened my eyes again. My eyelids felt heavier and heavier.

"Hey, Tessa, you remember when you used to bring your records over? Remember when we used to dance to this song?"

"Yeah, I remember."

"Let's go dance, come on." I stood up, wobbly, and bumped into something tall.

"Watch it!" Dave was the tall thing I'd bumped into. His drink had gone all over him. "Jeez, Johnny, control yourself!"

"Don't mind me, Dave-o, I'm just dancing with

your wife." I took Tessa's hand. "Come on, for ol' time's sake."

She patted Dave on the arm and followed me out to the dance floor.

We were dancing the way we used to, back in our old living room, on the old brown carpet. Our feet shuffling. She was still a spider-girl. It was just like it was. Like nothing bad had ever happened.

Suddenly, a wave of black swelled up from the base of my spine to the front of my head. The floor seemed to tilt up and down again like a ship. The next thing I knew, the music had stopped and my mother was calling my name.

"Johnny? Johnny! He's waking up!"

My eyes felt gummy. How did everything get so white?

"Johnny! Can you hear me?"

Of course I can, Mom, I wanted to say, but my tongue was thick. I could tell she was pissed. I tried to close my eyes again.

"Ma'am, we're going to need you to wait outside—" I got my eyes all the way open. An out-of-focus doctor showed my mother the door.

"Thanks." My voice came out a scratch. The doctor smiled and suddenly jerked my head around, peering a little pen light into my eyes. I squinted. That light was like the fucking *sun.*

"Try to keep your eyes open," he demanded, swirling the light around. Was this guy trying to blind me?

"You're a lucky young man," he announced finally. "Do you know what you took?"

"Um . . ." Thinking fast was not an option. "I just asked this girl for an aspirin."

"She didn't give you an aspirin." He gave me a perturbed look. "Was she a friend of yours?"

"A friend of a friend."

"Whoever you were with tonight left you outside the emergency room on the sidewalk. They drove off without even making sure you were all right." He clicked off his light. "If I were you, I'd seriously reconsider calling those people your friends." My mother came in as he was leaving. "I'll have Dr. Rubenstein down in a minute," he told her. She nodded and I could see her eyes were getting all glassy with tears.

"Mom—"

Her look shut me up. I couldn't tell if she was

about to bust out crying or kill me with her bare hands. She was still in her pajamas, with her jacket buttoned up wrong.

"I'm sorry," I whispered. She didn't cry, but she didn't smile and tell me everything was going to be okay, either.

Dr. Rubenstein turned out to be a shrink. She asked me all these questions about what kind of drugs I did, how many times a week, how old was I when I started, all that. Mom stayed in the room, looking out the window, and sometimes Dr. Rubenstein would look over at her, like she was double-checking. Mom would just shrug, or shake her head, like "I had no idea." Which she didn't. I was pretty careful. Well, I kept it together more than most. I knew better than to show up at school reeking of it, too drunk to walk.

Next came the cop, and I won't bore you too much about him. Cops ask the same question five different times, like you don't understand it the first time but if he rephrases it, you'll suddenly smack your forehead and go, "Oh! Of course, it was some chick named Stephanie! Let me give you her number!" I didn't even know her last name.

Of course, considering what the doctor said about them dumping me at the emergency room, maybe I should've tried sending a little cop hassle their way. I couldn't do it, though. I understood why they left me. They didn't want the club to get shut down, or to get in trouble themselves. I probably would've done the exact same thing. I was kind of surprised that Tessa didn't stay with me, but Dave had had some drug problems himself a few years before—maybe he wanted her to stay out of it. Anyway, I wasn't going to be a snitch.

So, the doctor talked to the shrink, the shrink talked to the cop, and they all talked to my mom, and she broke the news. They couldn't put me in jail, since I didn't have any drugs on me when I came in, but I was being sent to the next best thing—rehab. I guess I should've been pissed off, but I was kind of relieved, in a way. Nobody should be an alcoholic before the age of seventeen. And, though I didn't know it at the time, Parkwood Rehabilitation Center would change my life. And not just because of the twelve-step program. At Parkwood, for the first time, I heard Debbie Harry singing in French.

Sunday Girl

It was 6:37 A.M. on a Sunday at Parkwood. I was lying awake in my bed, waiting for the seven A.M. wake-up call. It was those early mornings that I wanted to drink, not Friday or Saturday night like you'd expect. Sundays were especially nostalgic for me. I would look up at those blaring white ceilings, painfully clear-headed, remembering all the mornings I used to wake up beneath the palm trees after passing out on the concrete, one hand dangling in the freezing water of Terry's swimming pool. There, the mornings came into focus slowly and with a friendly pink haze. If you were feeling rough from the weekend's activities, you could always stumble over to the cooler or the poolhouse and manage to find a near-empty beer can that didn't have a cigarette butt in it, or a mouthwash-sized swirl of vodka still lingering in somebody's cup. Those were the good times. So far, a life of sobriety seemed none too thrilling.

However, on this particular Sunday morning, a voice interrupted my daydreams of tequila and Jell-O shots. It was a female voice, soft and high-pitched, coming from somewhere just outside my room.

I padded out into the hallway in my sock feet. In the rec room, an older girl named Julia sat alone next to the radio, holding a cigarette out the window and reading *Vogue*. Julia was a lesbian with pierced eyebrows and pink hair who had started out a boozer and got herself hooked on a variety of hard drugs. Rumor had it that her parents had some shrink try to electroshock the lesbian out of her, but a lot of rumors floated around Parkwood.

At that moment, I was transfixed. Not with Julia,

but with the woman on the radio. She was singing in French. *"Dépêches-toi, dépêches-toi et attends."* I imagined her as a cross between Jean Seberg from *Breathless* and the St. Pauli Girl. I wanted that voice to sing to me forever.

"Siddown, Goth Boy," Julia hissed. "You're gonna get us caught." The rule was no TV, no radio, no noise before seven A.M.

"Who is this?" I huddled down in the seat next to Julia.

"Debbie Harry."

"Debbie Harry? The *Electric Youth* chick?"

"No, spaz. That's Debbie *Gibson*." She rolled her eyes and took a drag off her cigarette. They put patches on all the smokers at Parkwood, but everyone just pulled them off and snuck smokes in the shower. Julia snuck smokes anywhere she damn well pleased. "I thought you knew about music. Haven't you ever heard of Blondie?"

"I thought they were disco."

"They're so *not* disco." She rolled her eyes. "They're like punk. Well, they started off punk and then they were New Wave." The song ended, and the DJ came on and told us that we were listening to an

All-Eighties Weekend and we'd just heard Kajagoo-goo followed by "Sunday Girl," by Blondie.

"She sounded beautiful." I suddenly felt embarrassed that I'd said that out loud.

"She *is* beautiful, spazboy." Julia tossed her cigarette butt out through the bars on the window. She closed her *Vogue* and got up, taking the radio with her.

The next few days dragged by. On Wednesday, we had this stupid group visit to the beach, where all I got was hit on the head with a Frisbee. I kept twirling the dial on my Walkman, trying desperately to catch a Blondie song on the radio, but the All-Eighties Weekend was over. I kept thinking of that voice. *Dépêches-toi, dépêches-toi et attends.* Hurry up, hurry up and wait. French was my favorite class in school.

Then, on Thursday, Julia sat down next to me in the cafeteria. "I was looking for you yesterday," she said.

"I had to go to the beach."

"Bummer. Well, here. I made you something." She handed me a cassette. *The Best of Blondie.*

"Thanks." I clutched the tape, feeling like I'd just been handed contraband.

"No sweat. Keep it real, spazboy." She picked up her tray and was gone.

I was finally over the halfway point at Parkwood. It got easier and easier to sit through the group talks, to tell the counselors what they wanted to hear and actually mean it. I even made it through Family Day with my mom, gritting my teeth and apologizing to her for being irresponsible and all that crap. She took my apology without expression, like I was writing her a parking ticket.

And on those last few Parkwood Sunday mornings, instead of fantasizing about beer dregs, I slipped on my headphones and listened to Blondie. Listening to Debbie Harry sing the French part of "Sunday Girl" was somehow more reassuring than anything the counselors had told me so far. Maybe it was subliminal messages. Or maybe the shrinks were right. They kept telling me I was acting out with my clothes and music and especially my drinking to fill the void and ease the pain of my dad dying, and to get my mom's attention. I thought they were full of it—I probably would've turned out a scary-dressing drunk whether my old man was alive or not. But if they were right, and drinking eased the pain before, maybe Blondie could do it for me now.

On the day before I left Parkwood, Julia brought me a picture of Debbie Harry from an old *Rolling Stone.*

"See?" she said. "I told you she was hot."

And just like that, the St. Pauli Girl was history.

X Offender

Terry was being weird.

"So, like . . . what's the deal with your hair?" We'd been in Goodwill for almost twenty minutes before he said anything. "Did they make you do it? In, uh . . . Parkwood?"

"No. I just . . . wanted something new, I guess." I'd cropped my carefully grown tresses close to my head, with just a little cowlick sticking up in the back. "You think it looks okay?"

"It's all right." He shrugged, flipping through a rack of coats.

"I thought it kind of made me look more like Clem Burke."

"Who?"

"The drummer from Blondie," I reminded him.

"Oh." I'd been trying to witness the Blondie gospel to Terry, but he didn't seem interested. The summer was almost over, and I felt like I'd been locked in a time capsule or something. I'd missed everything. Terry had started dating Stephanie and had gotten a part-time job at Fast Foto, the camera place in the mall, so we'd barely seen each other since I'd gotten home. Plus, Mom didn't want me hanging out with him—she said his mom didn't supervise us enough. That was the point, of course.

"What do you think?" I held up a black and gray tie, not quite skinny enough, but close.

"It's all right." Terry barely looked away from the mirror. He was trying on a velvet jacket with a rip in the sleeve. Some of his arm spikes poked out of the tear.

"How about this one?" I held up another tie.

"Yeah, it's good, man." He wasn't even looking. I was getting annoyed. Terry was giving me the brush-off like I was—well, like I was exactly what I was. The kid who couldn't handle his shit. The one who got caught.

"Hey, am I boring you here?" I wanted everything to be cool between us again. For us to just hang out and have a good time.

"Do I look bored?" Terry took off the velvet jacket.

"We haven't even seen each other all summer, and now you're acting like it's this huge drag to hang out with me or something." I guess I was being melodramatic, but I didn't care.

Terry just stared at the jacket in his hands.

"I'm not keeping you here. You can go, if you're so miserable, or whatever."

"Look, I know you just got out of"—he looked around and lowered his voice—"Parkwood and everything, but it's like, I dunno, you don't seem like yourself."

"Well then, who do I seem like?" I demanded.

"I don't know! All the—the short hair and the weird clothes and the Blondie stuff—it's like—you're all—you're just acting different, that's all." Terry grabbed his stuff and went off to a pants rack in the back of the store. I paid for my ties and walked out to the parking lot. Then I walked back in.

"Sorry, I forgot something," I told the clerk, who was giving me a curious look.

I went straight back to the dressing rooms and identified Terry's feet beneath the curtain. I yanked back the tatty tweed fabric.

"Hey!" Terry was standing there in just his pants, shirtless and pale.

"Maybe I don't seem like myself, but here's a news flash." I couldn't control what came out of my mouth next. I just went off. "I got totally harassed by the cops over what happened at the Tower, and I coulda told them about you and Stephanie and the whole thing, but I didn't. Even though I know you took me to the hospital and you just left me there. So, put that in your pipe and smoke it, asshole." I let go of the curtain and stormed back out into the parking lot, everybody in Goodwill looking at me.

I started walking, not caring where, just walking away. I walked beneath the highway, through good neighborhoods with green lawns where soccer moms stared nervously at me, through bad neighborhoods with weedy lawns where dogs tethered by heavy chains barked and growled at me. I walked past trailer parks and condos, barely noticing the changes.

Terry was my best friend, and it was like all of a sudden we were speaking two different languages. I didn't know how to explain it to him—the difference between what I felt before and now. Before Parkwood, before Debbie, before I cut all my hair off, everything seemed so serious. Everything was a drag. I wanted to see how far I could go, if I could get away, *all the way,* and I saw it. I went to the edge and looked over. Terry and some of the other Goth kids I knew were always talking about death in a weird, detached kind of way. They were hooked on it, but in a cartoon way. It was like they wanted a zombie-movie version of it, not the real, messy, emergency-room version. I thought like that, too, for a while. But something changed, and I couldn't think that way anymore.

The people at Parkwood said something like this would happen. That people who had a "near-death experience" usually gained a renewed sense of life. I thought it was bogus, at first, but there I was. Mr. Happy-Go-Lucky all of a sudden. I realized I didn't want to sit around in a dark room, in love with being in the dark. I wanted some new kind of energy. I wanted something good to happen for a change. Maybe that made me sound like a crystal-toting hippie, but so what? Drugs didn't make me happy. Drinking didn't make me happy. Dancing to Blondie, on the other hand, made me feel all right. I thought about Terry finding me at lunch that day in freshman year. He sized me up, my clothes, my music, my attitude, and he decided I passed some test. Now my clothes, my music, and my attitude had changed. And I had failed.

I guess I should've hated him. But I didn't. I could see too clearly from his side. I was trouble. I officially had a "drinking problem." Now I was someone to look after, to worry about. I wasn't any fun. Not his kind of fun, anyway.

I kept walking until I wound up at the beach. My dad used to go to the beach sometimes after work. He'd stay out until dusk, swimming for hours against the tide before he came back and fell asleep without even eating. I just sat on the sand for a while, watching the waves until it was almost dark, and then I walked all the way home.

Mom was in the kitchen, putting a meat loaf in the oven.

"You were not to leave this house without telling me." She didn't even look up.

"I just went to Goodwill." I held up my bag of skinny ties. "See?"

"That's not the point!" She slammed the oven door. "Who drove you? Terry?"

"So what if he did? You wanna give me a Breath-alyzer or something?" I had just calmed down from fighting with Terry, and now she was getting me mad again.

"There is no need for your smart mouth!"

"Well, there's no need for you to freak out when I didn't do anything wrong!" I stormed off to my room.

"That's it. You're grounded!"

"I can't go anywhere, anyway!" I slammed my door. Damn! I was pissed. First Terry, then her. Sometimes I almost wished I was back in Parkwood.

A few days later I woke up early, before Mom left for work. I went to the kitchen and poured myself a bowl of Rice Chex. In her bedroom down the hallway,

Mom was on the phone. I opened the fridge for the milk and thought I heard my name. Maybe I was just getting paranoid. I tiptoed across the kitchen and strained to listen.

"Lorraine, I think it really will do him a world of good."

She was definitely talking about me.

"Ever since he started high school, he's been impossible, and now I just can't control him anymore. . . . I mean, I'll miss him, of course, but I honestly think it's for the best. . . ."

I had a prickly feeling in my head as I sat down to eat. Why was she going to miss me? I felt like I was pouring the milk in slow motion. Was she sending me back to Parkwood? To military school? My hands were sweating. She hung up the phone and came into the kitchen.

"Oh!" She jumped. "You're up early."

"Why'd you say you're going to miss me? Are you sending me back to Parkwood?"

"We'll discuss it tonight, John. I have to get to work."

"You had time to discuss it with Aunt Lorraine. Why can't you discuss it with me?" I pushed my chair back and glared at her. She looked away, rubbing the back of her neck.

"Johnny, you're getting older. I'm working all the time. I can't look after you—"

"You don't have to look after me." My voice sounded a little pleading. I was nervous.

"I've talked to Dr. Pritkin at Parkwood. We think it might be the best thing for you to be removed from tempting situations and people, like Terry." She took a deep breath. "So I'm sending you to South Carolina, to live with Uncle Sam—"

"What?" I stood up, my chair screeching out behind me. "You're *sending* me—"

"I think it's the best thing! It's quieter, the school is one of the best in the Southeast, and you'll have a good male influence—"

"I don't need a fucking male influence!"

"John! Watch your language!" My *language*? I didn't care if she was mad. I was madder.

"You can't just send me off on a whim because it's more convenient for you! You didn't even ask me first! I'm capable of making my own decisions— hell, I made decisions for the both of us after Dad died!" She looked at me, her lips tight.

"You showed how capable you were at decision making when you *decided* to take drugs, didn't you?" There was no arguing. Her voice was pure steel.

"I've set it all up." She picked up her purse and her briefcase. "I booked you on a train leaving next week. You'll start school up there on the thirtieth."

"Mom!" I felt like crying. She was really just going to ship me off.

"I have to go. We'll discuss this further tonight, when you've had a chance to think it over."

"I've thought it over! I don't want to leave!" The desperation in my voice was embarrassing. I sounded like a little kid who didn't want to go to the doctor.

"Look, it's going to be hard for me, too. But I want to do the best thing for you." She fumbled with her keys. "I'm sorry, John. I have to go."

I slumped down at the table. I just sat there for the longest time, and then I remembered my cousin Bug. We were playing Chutes and Ladders. That was when I overheard Mom telling Aunt Lorraine that she wanted Uncle Sam to leave because he reminded her too much of Dad. Now she was sending me off, too. I got up and looked in the bathroom mirror, trying to find traces of him in my eyes, my mouth, my bones. I didn't see anything but a skinny, short-haired kid who'd gone bad somehow, a package she didn't want, being returned to sender.

That afternoon, I sucked it up and called Terry. I apologized for going off on him at Goodwill and told him I was getting shipped off. He didn't seem to care. He was pretty stoned, though.

"Maybe you'll get to tip some cows or something," Terry offered.

"Huh?"

"In South Dakota. Don't they have a lotta cows?"

"No, dude, South *Carolina*. You gotta help me get out of this."

"Well . . . you can tip cows in South Carolina, too." His call-waiting clicked, and it was Stephanie.

"Hang on, man, I gotta take this."

"It's okay. I gotta go anyway."

"Yeah, well, listen, come by the house on Friday night. I'm having a party—we'll get fucked up together for old time's sake."

"I can't make it. Thanks anyway." He had already

clicked over to Stephanie. I chewed my fingernail and dialed the only other person I thought could help.

"Good afternoon, Right Round Records."

"Hi, Tessa, it's Johnny."

"Johnny, hi, I've been meaning to call you!" Her voice leapt at least an octave. "I heard about you going to Parkwood. That sounds like a total bummer."

"Yeah, um, listen, I've got a problem. My mom wants to send me to live with my uncle Sam in South Carolina—"

"You have an uncle Sam?" She laughed.

"Yes, see, the thing is, she won't listen to me, she just made this decision, and I was wondering if you could talk to her, you know, tell her that I'm changing my ways, and maybe, you know, because you're older, she'll listen to you." I was nearly out of breath.

Tessa didn't say anything. I could hear tinny music playing in the background, and the cash register opening and closing.

"I don't know. . . ."

"Just give her a call. You don't have to do anything."

"Johnny, maybe it'll be good for you. I mean, I'd totally go if I were you."

"What?" I couldn't believe what I was hearing.

"Johnny, do you know how messed up you were that night? You were totally gone."

"So why didn't you come with me to the hospital?" My voice sounded like a little kid's.

"You know why." She sighed, as if she were disappointed in me. "Dave and I just took over the store—we've got loans, mortgages—it's tough enough getting bankers to take us seriously without the cops breathing down our necks."

"I know." I'd already given up.

"Don't worry, Johnny. You're a good kid, you'll be fine with your uncle. It'll probably be really good for you. You can start fresh in a new school! You can be whoever you want."

"Yeah. I gotta go." I hung up the phone just as she was saying good-bye.

Just Go Away

South Carolina was disgusting. It pissed rain. Rain so heavy and dark it seemed black. The trees were so wet they looked black, too. And the trees were every-where—not the palm trees I was used to, but big, hulking, leafy things, all crowded together. No tall buildings, no beaches. Just a crummy little strip mall of a town and all these trees. I felt like I was lost in the woods.

"Well, Johnny, here we are." Uncle Sam pulled into the driveway of a huge, angular house surrounded by a near forest.

"Nice place," I mumbled.

"Thanks. I designed it." Sam was an architect. Real smart guy. And rich. He was on the board of Langley Prep, this school that he'd designed a new gym for. So, lucky me, I got enrolled at a discount.

"There you go." Sam opened the back door and Bug, now eleven, climbed out. So far she hadn't said a word to me. Even though Sam reminded her about the time we played Chutes and Ladders. Now she just scampered toward the house as fast as her little stick legs would go.

"She'll warm up," Uncle Sam told me as he popped the trunk. "She's anxious to get back to her rockets."

"Rockets?" I lifted two of my bags.

"Model rockets. Her latest passion." He took the third bag and closed the trunk. Uncle Sam took wide strides across the lawn as the rain dripped, with me trotting along behind him.

Inside, it seemed even bigger—modern, full of space and exposed roof beams. There was a skylight. It was like something out of one of those house magazines they have in dentists' offices. I followed my uncle up the stairs as he pointed out the rooms.

"This one's yours. You can fix it up however you want." He set my bag down at the foot of a huge bed. It was like a hotel room, just a bed, desk, bureau, and nightstand, but it was gigantic. My old room seemed like a closet in comparison.

"Thanks." I was still holding my bags. I felt kind of like I should tip him. Instead I squeezed water out of my hair. "Does it always rain like this?"

"It'll pass—it's just a summer storm. Are you hungry?"

"No, I'm fine right now, thanks." We both stood there awkwardly in the huge room, him in his flannel shirt and Dockers, me in my turquoise suit. *Okay, Sam, start Male Role Modeling so I can go home,* I thought.

"Well, if you do get hungry, just make yourself at home. We'll have dinner around seven."

"Okay. Thanks," I said again. He kept standing there. He was taller and lankier than my dad. Sometimes it was hard to remember they were brothers.

"Johnny, your mom told me about the problems you had back in Florida, and, well, I'm no great disciplinarian, but I do have a little girl to raise here. I know you're a good kid. Just keep me aware of your whereabouts, let me know if you're having friends over, and be in by eleven on weekends, seven on school nights. Except if it's a school activity or if you clear it with me first. And of course no alcohol or drugs. Sound fair?"

"Yes, sir." Not too bad. My curfew at home was ten.

"All right. That's my speech." He clapped his hands together and exhaled. "There are some papers from your school on the bed. I'll be downstairs if you need me."

"Okay." Outside, thunder cracked. I jumped.

"Don't worry," Uncle Sam reassured me. "It'll clear up after a while."

I nodded as he left. My school. Gross. I ripped the Amtrak tags off my bags and unzipped them. Inside the largest was a cardboard tube. I pulled out the poster inside, rolled it out flat on the bed. Before I left, I'd found at a garage sale this huge color close-up of Debbie. I couldn't believe my luck. It made me happier, to think about finding Debbie Harry in a garage on a warm, sunny Florida morning. I looked outside—what a view. More trees and more rain, coming down even harder now.

"Hi," a small voice said. I looked up. Bug was in my room.

"Hi," I said back. "How's it going?"

She shrugged. "Are you gonna live here a long time?"

"I dunno." I sure hoped not.

"Why'd you have to move in with us?"

"Because my mom made me."

"Oh." Bug kicked at the doorway. "My mom makes me do stuff I don't want to all the time."

"Yeah, it's a drag." I was unpacking, not really paying attention to the kid.

"Who's that lady?" She pointed at Debbie.

"That's Debbie Harry. She's a singer."

Bug was quiet for a while, watching me unfold my T-shirts. "Do you like space?"

"You mean like . . . astronauts and stuff?"

She nodded.

"Well, I used to live down in Florida, so our school took us on a trip to the Kennedy Space Center one time." I thought her eyes were going to pop out of her head.

"Did you see a shuttle launch?"

"Not in person. We just went to the museum and saw some of the old launchpads and stuff."

"What was it like?"

I thought back. Terry and I had just discovered

Jägermeister. During one of the lectures, we snuck off to the Rocket Garden to sit in one of the replica Apollo capsules and get drunk. We ended up tossing our cookies behind a Mercury 7 exhibit.

"It was awesome," I told her.

"Cool," she said. "You wanna see my rockets?"

"Okay." I abandoned the T-shirts.

Might as well go see the kid's rockets. Didn't have anything better to do.

That night, Sam made dinner for me and Bug. Bug was sulking and whiny, just pushing her food around her plate. We'd gotten along pretty well that afternoon, but maybe now she was starting some kind of sibling rivalry thing. I wondered if my mom would take me back if Uncle Sam thought I was a bad influence on his daughter.

"Come on, Bug. They'll be here at eight."

"I don't wanna go. Can't I stay here tonight?"

"You want to see your mom." Uncle Sam made it sound more like a command than a question.

"Yeah," Bug said. "But I don't wanna see Ro-ger." She drew his name out sarcastically. Uncle Sam sighed.

"I know, honey. But he's not a bad guy. Trust me, when you get older, you'll appreciate the time you spent with your mom."

I couldn't believe it. Sam's wife leaves him for some oily doctor, and he's cool about the whole thing.

"He smells like medicine. And he always keeps the TV on the Weather Channel." I could tell Uncle Sam was trying to keep from grinning.

"Maybe he likes maps," I said. Both of them looked at me. I felt a hot blush creeping up my neck, knowing I'd just said something completely moronic in the middle of a conversation I had no part in. Luckily, Bug laughed, and then Sam. We all relaxed. Bug started eating, and the doorbell rang.

"That's your mom. Run and get your bag," Sam told her. Bug rolled her eyes and made a big show of dragging herself upstairs. Uncle Sam sat there. The doorbell rang again.

"Do you want me to get that?" I offered. Sam shook his head adamantly.

"No, no. We've got a system. Connie rings the bell a couple of times, then she goes back and sits in her car. I don't see her if I can help it."

"Oh," I said finally. "Well. It's nice that you're, uh, on good terms about it."

"You think I did all right?" Uncle Sam asked. "I figure it's better if Bug works out how she feels about her mother and Roger on her own. Connie cheated on me, not Bug."

I was surprised. Not only was Uncle Sam even cooler than I had originally thought, he was asking my advice.

"Yeah, that's cool. My best friend, Terry, in Florida, his parents were divorced, and his mom always used to talk smack about his dad right in front of him. Terry used to get really bummed about it, even though he kind of thought his dad was a jerk, too."

Uncle Sam nodded like I'd imparted some sage wisdom. "I try not to make her pick sides, but sometimes it's easier said than done." He shook his head. Just then, Bug came trudging back in. She gave Sam a desperate little hug.

"Bye, Dad. See you Sunday."

"All right. Have fun, honey." He hugged her back. Bug was just a little girl with a dumb Star Wars backpack on, but I felt a weird kind of jealousy toward her right then. I wished I could hug my dad, or Uncle

Sam, or anybody right then, even my mom. It was a dumb thought, and I tried to chase it out of my head. I guess I was staring off into space or something, because Uncle Sam gave me a funny look.

"You okay, Johnny?"

"Yeah, no problem." I put a forkful of rice into my mouth.

"Looks like it's just you and me tonight. Maybe we can watch a ball game or rent a movie or something, huh?"

"Sure." I shrugged. Watch a ball game? Was he serious?

"Or if you want to get settled in, have some time to yourself, that's fine, too." A funny thought hit me all of a sudden, and I sat back in my chair. There was Uncle Sam, an old guy in a flannel shirt, and me, a kid in a skinny necktie, and both of us were doing the same thing—trying to pretend we weren't lonely as hell.

"A movie sounds like fun," I said. He nodded, and we finished our dinner in silence.

The next week, I started at Langley Prep. I rode an old ten-speed of Uncle Sam's that he'd fixed for me.

I modified my ultra-dorky school uniform, tight-rolling the pants so they looked pegged. I rolled up the blazer sleeves, flipped up the shirt collar, and loose-knotted the tie. Throw in my new black Chuck Taylors and it wasn't too bad.

First period was Algebra 2. Good to get it out of the way early. Then Biology, where we would be dissecting things, so that was kind of interesting. Next was European History with Mrs. Walker, an old battleax who gave me a dirty look when I walked in and an even dirtier one when I raised my hand in the roll call.

Then came Study Hall, which was a good excuse to catch up on the latest *Rolling Stone* magazines that the kids from the previous Study Hall ripped off from the library and left stuffed in the desks. Then lunch—being new, I ate alone. The afternoon was a breeze. English 11 with Mr. Jeffries, who seemed really laid-back and cool, and then French 3 with Mademoiselle Sheffield, who was fresh out of teaching school but spoke fluent French and had a groovy Jean Seberg hairdo to boot. And, this semester, no gym. All right. I decided I could deal.

And then there was Maria.

Kung Fu Girls

"So how was your first week?" Uncle Sam asked over dinner on Friday.

"Not too bad." I shrugged.

"Lot of homework?" He passed me the green beans.

"I've had worse."

"Are you making any friends?" Judy asked, refilling Bug's lemonade. Bug scowled. Judy was Uncle Sam's girlfriend.

"It's only been a week." I stuffed my mouth full of salmon so I wouldn't have to answer anymore. All I'd gotten in the friend department were funny looks in the hallways and people scurrying to leave if I tried to sit with them in the cafeteria. And someone had vandalized my locker during the Back-to-School dance, but I was trying not to take it too personally. I figured it was just new-guy initiation—truthfully, I was more appalled that the DJ kept Garth Brooks and Shania Twain in heavy rotation, and line dancing had occurred.

I could already tell there were two types of students at Langley Prep. There were the classic prep-school kids from old-money Southern families whose fathers and fathers-before-them came through the hallowed halls and all that crap. I couldn't figure them out—they were all fairly rich guys, with the same last names as the major roads, businesses, and private hospitals in town. But instead of spending their money on sports cars and designer clothes, like you'd think, they all drove big camouflage-painted trucks plastered with rebel flags. They traded turkey calls and Skoal cans in the hallways. Even stranger, despite their resemblance to dyed-in-the-wool rednecks, the only kind of music they liked, besides country, was gangsta rap. They were on some weird urban-noble-savage trip, I guess.

Then there were the fuck-ups, kids like me who had screwed up somehow, gotten held back or even kicked out of public school. Through influence or money, they were taken in by Langley Prep and subsequently whipped into shape. It didn't take a week to tell that the latter half were total shit in the eyes of the former.

And I could tell right away that Maria was a fuck-up, like me.

She had a schedule mix-up, so she wasn't in any of my classes until Tuesday, when she showed up for Walker's History and then Sheffield's French. She came in wearing combat boots with her school uniform. I don't mean Doc Martens like some of the other rebel girls, who thought they were all tough but still had their nails done like everybody else. I'm talking real-live army boots that went halfway to her knees. Old ones, too; the right one was reinforced with duct tape. She had tangled black hair that looked like it saw a comb maybe once a week if it was lucky, and she was so tall that her plaid skirt ended up hitting her midthigh, like a mini. She had a real jive walk, and instead of taking notes in class, she hid a book under the desk and read, still managing to look studious. She was smart in French, but in History I could tell Walker didn't like her, either. She'd ask Maria these trick questions to see if she was paying attention and always check to see if she had her homework. And, somehow, Maria always had the right answer and her homework completed. It was like she was rebelling by *not* being a delinquent.

Plus, when Mademoiselle Sheffield asked her name, she introduced herself as "Maria Costello. As in Elvis."

I dug her immediately.

A Brief History of Me and Girls: I had a lot of girl friends. (Note the space between those words.) Every time I thought I had a good thing going with a girl, she'd end up giving me that speech: "Johnny, I really like you . . . as a *friend*." I almost lost my virginity to this girl Kristen about a year ago. She used to hang out at the Tower and looked like Courtney Love (back when Courtney was chubby and cute). And she dressed like Stevie Nicks. She came to one of Terry's parties, and we fooled around most of the night, but in the end we just ended up passing out in the poolhouse. The next morning, I accidentally puked on one of her shawls. She never called back.

So I was nervous about talking to Maria. It wasn't just that I was on unfamiliar turf. There was something about her—you just couldn't picture her with a *boyfriend.* I mean, not that she was ugly or anything—she was really cool and exotic looking, even with her messy hair. But she was kind of aloof, like it would be stooping for her to date any guy at our school, especially me.

So when she stopped by my locker one Wednesday afternoon, it goes without saying that I was pretty surprised.

"Hey," she said. She leaned up against the locker next to mine.

"Hi," I said, twirling my combination lock. My locker combination had just been erased from my memory, along with my ability to speak the English language.

"I'm Maria."

"Costello. As in Elvis," I said. She smiled. I made her smile! "I'm Johnny McKenzie. As in, uh . . ."

"Spuds?" She grinned. I felt myself blushing.

"Sure," I replied feebly. *Spuds MacKenzie? The Beer Dog? Great.*

"I thought your history report was awesome," she told me. "It made me laugh."

"I'm glad somebody liked it," I told her. "Walker gave me a D."

"Don't sweat it. She's so uptight she thinks *Moby Dick* is risqué. She'll kiss your ass if your family's rich, though. Does your dad own a car dealership or anything?"

"No." I tugged on my locker, which was stuck, as usual.

"Ah, well." She waved her hands like she was shooing away gnats. "It's only a year."

"Yeah." My mouth was dry. I was grasping for snappy comebacks. I yanked my locker door—no dice.

"Here, look out." Maria pushed me gently back from the locker and gave it one good, hard thump with the heel of her hand. The door swung open like an oiled gate.

"Aaayyy." She grinned and leaned back against the other lockers, giving me the thumbs-up.

"Thanks." Now I really felt like a dumbass. This

girl was a female Fonzie, for Pete's sake. She was even cooler than Tessa, and when it came to girls Tessa was my Cool Standard.

"Mine does the same thing. What's with the plastic?" She was looking at the pictures in my locker, which I'd taped up in clear plastic sandwich bags.

"Vandals," I told her. When I'd gone to get my jacket after the Back-to-School dance, I found my locker half open, my jacket and books on the ground. Inside the locker, someone had written FAG in red permanent marker all across a picture of Robert Smith I had hanging beside my schedule. Even though I'd just ripped it out of a magazine, it pissed me off. So, when I found a good shot of Debbie, I turned to Ziploc.

"Is that Debbie Harry?" Maria stepped in for a closer look.

"Yeah. From Blondie." I remained calm. She knew Debbie Harry!

"Blondie. Right. '*Once I had a love . . .*'" she sang in a Bee Gees–worthy falsetto.

"Hey, not bad!"

"Come on." She rolled her eyes. "She's a Disco Cheesecake!"

Wait a minute. Did Maria really think that Debbie was just a *Disco Cheesecake*?

"Well, that was just one song." I was losing it. Burning up on re-entry. Houston, we have a problem.

Maria grinned. "You just think she's hot."

"I do not!" I protested, a little too loudly. Some kids down the hall turned and looked at me. *Shut up, you idiot! They already think you're gay! Recover, recover!* "I mean, sure, she's pretty hot and all; I'm not made of stone. But it's the music, you know—Debbie— Debbie Harry sings in French!" *Debbie Harry sings in French? That's the best you can do?*

"French, huh?" Maria had this amused look on her face. "Okay, well, I gotta run. Later on, Johnny." Suddenly, she was halfway down the hall.

"See you around?" I called after her pathetically.

"Yeah, see ya," she called back over her shoulder. She turned the corner and disappeared. The final bell rang, and I looked at Debbie.

"Thanks a lot," I muttered. She just pouted coolly at me from inside her plastic bag.

The Beast

The next Tuesday was our first dissection in Biology. Earthworms. I got paired up with a guy named Ben Woods, a huge rhinoceros of a senior who was repeating the class. He would've been another fuck-up but for his excellence on the wrestling mat, which, along with his easygoing demeanor, made him beloved.

"Man, I don't know if I can do this," he admitted as we pinned our earthworm to the dissection tray.

"It'll be all right. You've been fishing before, right?"

"Yeah." He gripped the scalpel. "But this is like

surgery or somethin'. I dunno, man. How 'bout you cut and I write?"

"Sure." I took the scalpel and stood in front of the worm.

"So where'd you move from?"

"Tampa, Florida." I made the first incision.

"Oh, sweet. You ever go to the Daytona 500?"

"No, I've never been too much of a NASCAR fan, myself."

"Really? You surf down there?"

"No. Tampa's not really good for surfing. You wanna observe the first incision, here?"

"Naw, man, I'm good. So what sports do you play?"

"I . . . um . . . run track." I'd never run track in my life, but I was a pretty fast sprinter in gym class, so I figured it was a lie I could get away with.

"Aw, that's gotta suck. Langley doesn't have a track team!"

I looked over at him. He seemed genuinely concerned for me.

"Yeah . . . I was really bummed. So, what's the first system we write about? Digestive?"

"Uh . . . yeah. . . ." Ben was turning pale.

"You okay, man?"

"Yeah, just not feeling too hot. . . ." Ben clamped his hand over his mouth and bolted for the door. I pulled off my rubber gloves and started taking notes on the digestive system of the *Lumbricus terrestris.*

Over the next week, Maria smiled in my direction a few times in class (which I felt pretty good about, since she didn't smile much in general), but we didn't get a chance to talk again. Which is to say, I never worked up the nerve to talk to her. No matter. This was the new and improved Me, a homework machine, getting into bed on time, eating healthy food, not skipping any classes. I was on the straight and narrow. So, on Thursday, when I got an envelope from my mother containing a Bible verse and a twenty-dollar bill, I went straight to the phone book to find a place to spend it.

I found Rocksteady Records in a mostly abandoned wood-paneled strip mall, along with a manicure shop and the grimy-windowed Rusty's Carolina B-B-Q. I chained my bike to a broken pay phone and went inside.

An old bell on the handle clanked as the door

shut behind me. The guy behind the counter was skinny and black, with long dreads and sunglasses. He gave me a nod. I nodded back. I'd come straight from school, so I was still in my uniform. There was a fast punk song playing. I took a look around.

This place was definitely cool. You could tell right away. There were posters on the wall of the Kinks and the Rolling Stones when they were young. It reminded me of Right Round Records—all vinyl, and everything was arranged by genre. I checked New Wave first, then Female Vocalists. Lots of Petula Clark, who looked interesting, but no Debbie.

"Excuse me." I went up to the guy with dreads. I suddenly expected him to laugh at me, and my throat tightened. "Do you know where I could find some . . . Blondie records?"

"Back wall. New York section." He had a cool accent, Southern and Jamaican at the same time. I went to the back wall and flipped through the bin. Sure enough, Blondie. They had the ones I already had, plus two others—*Plastic Letters* and one simply called *Blondie*. I could afford both, but I wanted to save something for later. I checked the back covers. I was trying to go chronologically, so *Blondie* it was.

The clerk looked at the record, front and back. "Ain't you kind of young for this?"

"Is it R-rated?"

"Maybe PG-13." He laughed. "Nah, man, it's a good record. You can't get it on CD, you know. The whole Blondie catalogue, out of print."

"Yeah." I handed him my money and he rang it up.

"You new in town?"

"Yeah. I used to live in Florida."

"Ah, the Sunshine State. I grew up near there."

"Really? Where?"

"Jamaica." He broke into a grin. "Where'd you think I was gonna say—Mobile, Alabama?"

I just shrugged.

"How did you end up in South Carolina?" I asked him.

"My dad's from here. How about you, why'd you move?"

"Bad luck," I said.

He laughed and handed me the record. "So you like punk music? New Wave?"

"I guess." I shrugged. "I like Blondie. I like the Ramones all right."

"You should go to the Village Green."

"What's that, another record store?"

"Nah. It's a club. They got a lot of punk bands, and it's usually all ages. If it's not, just tell the guy at the door you're a friend of mine. I'm Lucas." He offered his hand.

"Thanks. I'm Johnny." We shook.

"You got good taste in music, Johnny Ace. Maybe I'll see you around town."

"Yeah. Thanks." As I was leaving, I bumped right into these two barbeque-smelling, skate-punk guys. It took me a minute to recognize them because they'd changed their clothes, but they went to Langley Prep, and they were seniors.

"Sorry," I said, stepping out of their way.

"Move it, faggot," one of them said under his breath. "You got the new Limp Bizkit?" he yelled out to Lucas, rolling the toothpick from one corner of his mouth to the other.

"Nah, man. Try the mall," Lucas told them, his voice contemptuous. They brushed past me again on their way out the door. A clammy feeling ran through me, but I tried to push it away. *What would Terry do?* I thought. But I was too sober to bat my eyelashes at them.

Anyway, it was sticks and stones. I had plenty of stuff to be glad about, for once. I put the new Blondie record carefully in my backpack and unlocked my bike. I'd just met someone cool who invited me to a cool club, and I had two sides of pure Debbie to listen to when I got home.

(I'm Always Touched by Your) Presence, Dear

I decided to bite the bullet and ask Uncle Sam if I could check out the Village Green. He'd heard of it and told me that as long as it was an all-ages show and I finished my homework, I could go. Just like that. It would be my first night out since Tower—I would even take my real ID.

I spent Saturday doing algebra, reading about multicellular organisms for Biology, and listening to the first Blondie album. The songs were really rock-and-roll-y, and the band looked cool on the back cover. They all had cool clothes—Chris Stein's satin jacket that said "Rhythm Kings." Gary Valentine's tie. Jimmy Destri's jacket. Clem Burke's snazzy red trousers and black belt. And, of course, Debbie. Do women like this really exist? She was wearing a tight red-checked shirt that looked like a pizza parlor tablecloth and saddle shoes, but she somehow made it look like the sexiest outfit ever worn. They looked like the coolest bunch of people on the planet. Why couldn't I go to school with *them*?

Seven o'clock rolled around. I ate a sandwich and got dressed. Black pants, red dress shirt, black tie. I put on a little eyeliner and mascara and stuck my black Ace comb in my back pocket. ID, cash, change, keys, Trident spearmint . . . okay, I was ready to go.

The Village Green was kind of far, but I didn't mind. I rode out of the suburbs and into the town, which wasn't much of a town, just a suburb with businesses. I rode past the florists and the Hardee's and the hair places with names like Shear Elegance and Mane Street Salon. The evening air was cool, nice just to ride around in. The sun was almost gone—it was already getting dark earlier, and soon the leaves would be falling. Living in Tampa, I'd never really experienced winter, and I wasn't sure if I was looking forward to it or not.

I chained up my bike. The Village Green was in another half-deserted strip mall. There was a long line outside, a mix of punks and Goths and regular kids in jeans and sweatshirts. I told the guy at the door that I was a friend of Lucas. He waved me in.

Inside, the DJ played as the band set up. A banner above the stage read LADIES' NIGHT! It was nothing like the Tower—no black velvet drapes, no purple couches. The Village Green might as well have been a barn. The audience was scattered, talking, smoking, drinking beer out of plastic cups. I wanted a drink like mad, but I thought of Debbie instead. Tried to recite back all the songs on the new album. "X Offender." "Little Girl Lies." "In the Flesh."

"What's a nice guy like you doing in a place like this?" I turned around. It was Maria. She wore black pants, her black boots, a white shirt, and a black jacket. She had a cigarette perched between her long fingers. I tried to smile and play it cool. Like I came here all the time. Like my heart was beating normally and my mouth wasn't completely dry because suddenly she was standing there.

"Just hanging out. What about you?"

"Same." She puffed the cigarette. "Smoke?"

"No thanks."

"Did you just get here?"

"Yeah."

"Bummer—you just missed Janie Jones."

I wanted to sound cool, but I'd never heard of Janie Jones. "Does she go to Langley?"

"Um . . . no . . . Janie Jones is an all-girl Clash tribute band. But you're just in time for the Ramonas."

Okay, I was a dork. It looked like she was going to let me live. "Lemme guess—an all-girl Ramones tribute band?"

"That's why they call it Ladies' Night." She crushed her cigarette butt with the toe of her boot. "Come on, let's go get a spot up front." She yanked my hand and we made our way to the edge of the stage as the lights went down. The Ramonas came out, four lanky girls with dyed black hair hanging into their eyes, playing Ramones songs like nobody's business. They were good, and cute, too, even though they were pretending to be guys. Maria was singing along with every word, getting really into it. Everyone was pogo dancing, and before I knew it, I was pogoing with them.

The songs were fast and loud and I liked it. A mosh pit formed, and Maria and I shoved ourselves into the middle of it. We careened and caromed around, picking each other up as soon as we fell. I was sweating, and I could feel mascara running down my cheeks. I usually hated mosh pits, but tonight I didn't care. The music was good, and Maria was there. I felt loose and free, like when you're a little kid and you spin yourself dizzy until you can't stand up anymore.

The show ended. We went outside on wobbly legs, our ears throbbing. Maria howled like a wolf into the night.

"Now *that* was awesome!" She was jumping around. "I love coming out of a show like that! I feel like I'm high!" She looked at me—I was just watching her.

"Sorry." She tucked her hair behind her ear. "You probably think I'm nuts."

"No. It was an awesome show." *And I don't think you're nuts,* I wanted to say. *I think you're beautiful, wonderful, funny, smart—*

"So, are you doing anything now?" I asked. We were standing in front of my bike.

"I gotta get home. I have a curfew."

"Yeah, me too." She probably thought I was some total perv now, trying to put the moves on her or something. "I just thought, you know, if you wanted to get something to eat or something."

"Oh." There was the kind of silence that is never anything but awkward. She was no doubt figuring out a polite way to tell me to piss off when Lucas came out with a couple of punk girls, all pierced and rainbow-haired.

"Hey, Johnny Ace! You made it!" He turned to the girls. "First show at the Green."

"Oh, Lucas, this is Maria—"

"Ah, I think we've met." Lucas took her hand politely.

"Sure, you work at Rocksteady, right?"

"Rocksteady. Yeah." Lucas held her hand for a minute. He was giving her this weird look. I couldn't tell if he was putting the moves on her or what. Maria cleared her throat, and Lucas finally dropped her hand. "Well, I gotta take the ladies home. You kids have fun tonight!" Lucas walked off, his arms around the girls.

"So he's a friend of yours?" Maria looked at me.

"I met him in Rocksteady the other day."

"You shop at Rocksteady? Cool." She said *cool*. In reference to something *I* did. Was it possible that Maria Costello actually thought I was cool? "What'd you buy?"

"Huh?"

"What record?"

"*Blondie*. The debut album."

"Oh, right." She smiled. "You know, if a musically discerning guy such as yourself deems them worthy, I may have to rethink my position on the whole Blondie thing." Okay, now, not only was *I* cool in Maria's eyes, but she was coming around on Blondie, too?

"You should definitely check them out," I told her, trying to sound nonchalant.

"Hey, if you want to, we could go by the Needmore and get some food, or whatever," she suggested. "It's twenty-four hours. And I'll treat."

"Okay." I unlocked my bike and pushed it along as we walked. As she walked. And I walked next to her. Walking her home.

Maria was telling me about the real Ramones and Clash in between Icee slurps. We were walking through a suburb full of small houses near an old deserted textile mill. It kind of reminded me of a grungier version of my old Tampa neighborhood. The yards were scrubby red-clay squares, littered with toys and lawn ornaments like plastic deer and geese. Suddenly, Maria stopped in front of a tiny one-story house with nothing in the yard but some overgrown grass.

"This is my stop," she said. Not exactly where I imagined most private school kids coming from. "I know," she said. "It ain't exactly the Ritz. In case you're wondering, the only reason I go to Langley is because of my grandmother in Atlanta. She's got money coming out her ears, and she thinks young ladies of stature need a private school education." She put on a mock–Scarlett O'Hara voice.

"That's why I'm there," I remarked. She chuckled.

"Well, thanks for the walk." She sort of hit me in the shoulder. I had the strange feeling I wanted to tell her something, but I wasn't sure what.

"Thanks for the Icee." That was what I wanted to tell her?

"No prob. Later on, Johnny." She ran to the door and I could hear the lock click. I waited until the door closed, and, after a while, I saw a light go on in the front corner of the house. Must be her bedroom. I looked at that little rectangle of light for a long time before I finally got on my bike and pedaled away.

When I got home, Uncle Sam was waiting up in the den, leafing through *Architectural Digest.* He stifled a yawn as I came in.

"How was the show?"

"Great," I said.

"Open your mouth," he commanded.

"Excuse me?"

"You heard me. Open it."

Tentatively, I opened my mouth.

"Now stick out your tongue and give me an *aaah.*"

"Aaaah," I gurgled. He inhaled.

"Hm." He looked at me sternly. "It's blue. Am I going to have to call your mother and tell her that you've been flagrantly abusing sugary snacks?" I gave him a look—was he for real?

"I'm joking with you, John." He leaned over to switch off the desk lamp. "Actually, your mom did call."

"What did she say?" I caught myself tensing up.

"She just wanted to talk to you, see how school was going."

"Was she mad that I was out?"

"I told her you were at a friend's house studying for midterms."

"Thanks." At that moment, there was nobody on the planet cooler than my uncle Sam.

"She gets a little worked up sometimes. I figured I could trust you."

"I appreciate that." I didn't know how to say it so he'd know I was serious. "I really do. Appreciate that you trust me. I'm trying to be better."

"I know you are, John. But I can appreciate where your mom's coming from. She lost your dad. She doesn't want to lose you, too."

"She's got a funny way of showing it."

"Well, parents don't always make the right decisions." He sighed. "We're getting along, though. Right?"

"So far so good."

"All right, then. Hit the sack, Jack, and don't forget to brush your teeth."

"I won't. Thanks, Sam."

As I was scrubbing my face in the sink, I thought about Maria, and then about my uncle Sam. He had his moments. When he was joking around, he kind of reminded me of my father. Sometimes I wondered if he would've been a cool dad if he'd lived, or if we just would've fought all the time.

Well. No use thinking about stuff like that. I'd had a good night, and I was happy. I didn't want to start thinking about impossible things that would just make me sad.

Dreaming

I fell asleep thinking of Maria, but I dreamed about Debbie Harry. I was back at the Village Green, and when I went outside, she was standing beside my bike. She was smoking a cigarette and wearing a very dramatic outfit with a cape.

"Hi, Johnny," she said.

"Hi, Debbie," I said back. As if it were the most normal thing in the world to find Debbie Harry standing watch over your ten-speed.

"Nice threads," she told me.

"I like yours, too," I told her.

"How are things going with Maria?"

"Oh, you know." I shrugged.

"You should tell her how you feel. She likes you, too, you know."

"I don't know. She's so cool. And beautiful."

Debbie gave me a smile. "*Dépêches-toi,* Johnny," she said, taking a drag from her cigarette.

My eyes flew open. Now, I don't usually believe in dreams and stuff like that. But something about this one—Debbie seemed so vivid, it was like I could smell the cigarette smoke. And I knew I had to see Maria right then and tell her how much I liked her, which is what I wanted to tell her in front of her house just hours ago. I threw on my clothes.

It was two in the morning. I sped over to Maria's. When I got there, I just stopped in front of the house, suddenly feeling dumb. What was I going to do, ring the doorbell? Explain to her parents that Debbie Harry had just come to me in a dream and told me that their daughter and I were meant to be?

"This is ridiculous," I muttered. Just as I was deciding to leave, I heard something rustle in the bushes, near the window where I'd watched Maria's light go on. Maybe it was some animal. But then I heard voices. My heart quickened. I wanted to ride away as fast as I could, but I couldn't leave Maria to whatever—whoever—was in those bushes. I dropped my bike by the curb.

"Hey," I called out as I crossed the lawn. They ducked down to hide, whispering "Shh!" and "Who the hell is that?" There was more than one of them. What if they had guns, or if they were high and crazy? I crept closer and felt a strange sense of relief when I saw that it was those two guys from school. The ones I'd seen in Rocksteady. And Ben, my biology lab partner.

"Hey, I know him—" Ben said.

"Yeah, it's that fucking homo!" The voice sounded familiar. It was the same guy who'd asked for the Limp Bizkit record.

"Shit! Get out of here, faggot," another one of the bushes hissed at me.

"What the hell—" My relief was quickly turning into anger. As I got closer, I could see right in Maria's window. There was a dim lamp on, and she was still up. Her boots were on the floor, untied, one flopped over on its side. Her black jacket from earlier was laid out on the bed. All she was wearing was her white shirt, halfway unbuttoned. She had a record player on milk crates in the corner, and she was kneeling in front of a stack of records, looking for the right one. It was like some slightly pervy Norman Rockwell. Her bare thighs were pale, creamy white.

"What're you looking at, fag?" The one who'd just called me a homo was standing right in front of me. I could smell alcohol on his breath. Sour-sweet, like rum drinks.

"What're *you* looking at?" I repeated, sounding surprisingly intimidating. To myself, anyway.

"My girlfriend, that's what I'm looking at."

My heart thrashed. I wanted to kill him, and I think I would have, but there seemed to be no blood in my body all of a sudden.

"Fuck off, faggot." He breathed heavily. I got that clammy feeling again. Prickly fingertips.

"Don't call me—"

"What? Faggot?"

I lost it. I tackled him, and he went down. I don't know which of us was more surprised. I'd never been in a fight in my life. One of the other guys grabbed me, and the guy I'd just knocked down popped up like a kid's punching bag and slammed his fist into my jaw. I actually saw little stars, like when you close your eyes and press down on your eyelids. Everything went white, then black, and then a light came on, and it was Maria. She was standing on the tiny porch in a Japanese-style kimono. It was red satin, with what looked like little black dragons on it. She also had a shotgun balanced on her hip.

"What's going on out here?"

"Don't shoot!" The boyfriend held up his hands, staggering.

"I'm not going to shoot you, Brian. Donald, let him go." Donald must've been the thug holding me, because all of a sudden I was unsqueezed. I nearly sank to the ground, but I wavered and caught myself. Ben grabbed me.

"You all right, man?" He slurred under his breath.

"Yeah. Leggo." I pulled away from him. He'd just stood by while I was getting my ass kicked. Some friend.

"Johnny?" Maria recognized me. I opened my mouth to explain—

"We were just on the way back from Duffy's, and, uh, we saw this kid was looking through your window," Brian the Boyfriend said.

"What? That's a fucking lie!" My mouth stung when I spoke.

"Shut up, you little prick," Donald muttered. I whirled around, ready to kill him. He gave me a dangerous look.

"All right, enough!" Maria yelled. "Johnny, get over here." I obeyed sheepishly, noticing the way the kimono was starting to slip off her shoulder.

"You three, get out of here before I call the cops."

"Maria, come on—" Brian started.

"Leave!" She shifted the gun on her hip. They went skulking off. She turned to me and put her finger under my chin, looking at my face in the porchlight.

"You're bleeding," she told me. "Come on in." I followed her into the house. She locked the door. "Don't worry about being quiet, my dad works nights. He's a security guard. We've got Coors in the fridge, if you want one."

"I don't drink."

She put the shotgun in the hall closet and

smiled at me. "I don't either." She led me to her bedroom. It was cozy, with dark purple drapes and just the record player, a bed, a desk, and a bookshelf. There were stacks of books and magazines and records and CDs everywhere.

"You've got a lot of music."

"My grandmother keeps sending me money for clothes, and I keep blowing it all at Rocksteady." She shrugged. "Cheaper than most habits, and there's no hangover."

"Yeah," I agreed. She had no idea. "So is your mom—around?"

"No, she's not here." She sat me down on the edge of the bed. "I mean, she doesn't live with us. Stay right there. I'm gonna get you some ice."

For the first time with Maria, I felt cool. But, for the first time, I didn't feel like I had to be. She came back with a washcloth full of ice cubes and a bottle of peroxide.

"Tilt your head back." I did. She dabbed the peroxide on my mouth. I winced, and she blew lightly on my lips. I opened my eyes and looked at her.

"Maria, I swear, I came up on those guys trying to look in your window. I would never—"

"I know." She tightened the washcloth around the ice like a little fist. "Here." I put the cloth to my mouth. It was so cold it burned. "They were trying to get me to come out with them. I was hoping if I ignored them they'd go away." She went to the record player. "You like Nico?"

"I dunno." I looked over at the album she was putting on. *Nico: Chelsea Girl.* It had a picture of a sad-looking blonde on the cover. The first few notes came on—the music was nice.

"How come you're still awake?" I watched her stretch like a cat and stand up.

"Couldn't sleep. What about you? I thought you had a curfew." She sat down on the bed.

"I thought you did, too."

"My dad calls from work."

"Oh."

"So what's your story?"

"I had this dream."

"About me?" She smiled.

"Sort of." I tried to smile back, but my lips were numb. It was quiet for a minute, except for Nico.

"So that was your boyfriend?" I asked cautiously.

"Brian Quinn? He told you he was my boyfriend?"

Maria sat up and crossed her legs. "We used to hang around together. When I was here before. I mean, I'm supposed to be a senior this year. But I left last year, so they're making me repeat."

"Where did you go?"

"Manhattan."

"Wow. Why didn't you go to school there?"

"I dropped out. The school kind of sucked. I was living with my mom, and I got a job working for this strip club—"

"You were a stripper?" My voice went up really high, and I was immediately mortified.

"I just worked the coat check." She laughed, but it seemed halfhearted. Her eyes focused on the floor. "It's a long story. I'm going back for Christmas. I just have to get the money. My mom's kinda broke right now, and my grandmother—she's my dad's mom—she's mad at her for splitting up with my dad, so she won't help her out or give me any money to go see her. I have to save up on my own." She looked down and picked at the bedspread, then smoothed it out. I wasn't going to ask her any more, but she started talking again.

"Brian and I went out for most of tenth grade.

Things were really different then. I was kind of, I dunno, upset about a lot of things. Me and those guys kind of had that in common—we were all pissed off and bored, and we just wanted to be rowdy and mess shit up. It was fun for a while—it's not like there's anything else to do around here. I guess he wants things to be like that again. Just, you know, hanging out in the woods, getting high and breaking bottles. But I'm different, and he's different, too. He's more . . . hateful. Even to his friends."

I knew what she meant. Selfishly, I still hated the fact that she'd given this guy Brian the time of day, let alone—well, I didn't want to think about what else she'd given him.

"So what's your story? Where'd you come from?" she asked.

"Tampa."

"Florida. Cool. Did you live on the beach?"

"No, just the regular suburbs. Kind of like this neighborhood. But we were only about fifteen minutes from the beach."

"Nice. So why'd your family move?"

"I'm the only one who moved. I'm living with my uncle. My mom's still down there."

"What about your dad?"

"He died."

"Oh." She halted. "God, Johnny, I'm sorry."

"It's okay. I mean, it's not okay, but it's been a couple of years now. I'm not crying on my pillow every night."

"It's still tough, though, isn't it?" She looked at me.

"I guess." I could taste the blood from my lip. "Yeah."

"So how come you're not with your mom?"

I gave her the basic story.

"Geez, Johnny." Her eyes were big. "I saw a guy—a friend of mine in New York—he OD'd one time. You're lucky to be alive." Her voice had gotten quiet.

"I guess." I held the washcloth to my lips again. The white was turning a blotchy reddish brown.

"Was it coke, or junk, or what? I mean, do you mind me asking?"

"No, no—" She thought I was a drug addict. "I'm actually— I'm not sure what it was. This girl in a club gave me something and I'd been drinking a lot, and—it all sorta caught up with me."

"Oh." She cleared her throat. "So you nearly died and your mom sent you packing?"

"Yeah. Pretty much."

"My mom ditched me, too. Doesn't it piss you off?"

"Yeah." We both just sat there for a second, looking at each other. The music finally ended. Maria got up and flipped the record.

"She probably did you a favor," she said suddenly. "Making you leave Florida, I mean. Bad vibe central. That's where they nabbed Jim Morrison. And Patti Smith broke her neck down there. You're better off up here."

"You think so?" I gave a laugh that sounded more like a sigh. I missed being at home, but here was Maria saying I was better off up here. Where she was. Maybe she was right.

"Yeah. I can't believe you came over." She sat down on the floor. I couldn't really believe it, either.

"I've done crazier things." I held my breath. "Anyway, I like you."

"You do?" She sounded surprised. "Really?"

"Well, yeah. I like you a lot. I'm glad I saw you

tonight. I mean at the concert. And now, too."
Dumb. But she was smiling.

"Wow. No offense, but I thought you were gay."
Her too? Man.

"Well, contrary to popular belief, I'm not." I was
a little peeved.

"I mean, I don't care if you are or not." She got
up off the floor and sat next to me on the bed. "I'm
glad you're not, though. 'Cause I like you, too."

She liked me? She liked me! Okay, what's next?
Do I kiss her now? What?

"So, um"—she stood up—"you wanna play
Scrabble?"

We played two games, and she beat me both times,
once by adding a *y* to a word I'd already spelled, *fox*,
and landing on a triple word score. We listened to a
couple more albums, and she knew all these little
facts about them—who the producer was, who
went on to marry a supermodel, everything. She
told me that Chrissie Hynde from the Pretenders
had dated Ray Davies from the Kinks, and that Mick
Jagger wrote "Wild Horses" after Marianne Faithfull

woke up from a drug overdose and said, "Wild horses couldn't drag me away." I told her that after I woke up from my overdose, I just felt like puking. She laughed. Then, when the sun was up and it was almost time for her dad to come home, she walked me to the door.

"Thanks for the ice. And the Scrabble," I told her. "Sorry I got blood on your washcloth."

"No prob. Next time I might let you win." She kissed me on the cheek, and I reached for the porch railing, feeling like I was going to float away.

"Hey, Johnny!" she called out as I crossed the lawn.

"Yeah?" I called back.

"I'm glad you're not gay!"

Youth Nabbed as Sniper

On Monday, some of the kids at school stared at my cut lip, and I felt like a badass. I felt bad for lying to Uncle Sam—I told him I'd fallen during an early-morning bike ride and he bought it, but, in a weird way, I wished I could've told him I was in a fight. I was kind of proud that, even though I didn't exactly win, I'd taken a punch and hadn't even cried.

I could barely stay in my chair all day long. I kept thinking up things to tell Maria, smart things about rock and roll. Entire conversation topics with main points. Maybe I'd even invite her over to listen to my Blondie records. Yep, I was feeling good. My hair wasn't even doing a cowlick!

She told me to meet her by the bike rack after school. She'd just gotten her bike fixed, and we were going to ride to Rocksteady together and then go Goodwill shopping. I burst outside after the final bell. While the other kids scurried to unleash their bikes and get home, Maria was leaning against the rack, her long legs crossed in front of her. She was reading a book of Baudelaire poems and wearing sunglasses.

"Hi." She looked at me and scrunched her nose. "What's up with you?"

"I'm trying to decide whether you look more like a movie star or a really spectacular comic book archvillain." I tucked my hands in my pockets, on top of the world.

Maria laughed and grinned, baring her teeth. "Do you always talk like that?"

"Only when provoked." Or stupidly infatuated. "You still wanna ride out to Rocksteady?"

"Yeah, where's your bike?" She zipped the book away in her backpack.

"Right here by the—" I pointed to the end of the rack, but my bike was gone. The chain lay in two coils on the ground.

"Somebody took it." I stated the obvious.

"Are you kidding me? Somebody stole your bike?" She yanked off her sunglasses, looking outraged. "Damn!"

I picked up the two parts of the chain, a strange feeling in my chest.

"Looking for something?" I knew it. I turned around. There was Brian, holding my bike up high by the front tire. Donald stood close behind him.

"Oh, hi, Brian," I said, smooth as I could manage. "Where's the third stooge?"

"Shut up, faggot. You want this back?"

I felt hot prickles beneath my skin. "No, you can keep it."

He blinked, not sure of a comeback. Finally, he hoisted it up with both hands and threw it. Maria and I both ducked. The bike flew over our heads and smashed down in the trees behind us.

"Brian!" Maria exclaimed. "Who do you think you are, the Incredible fucking Hulk?"

"If I'd known you liked hanging around with queers"—Brian's chest heaved—"I never woulda wasted my time."

"But, Brian, why do you think I hung around with you?" She batted her eyes innocently.

"I don't know what the hell they did to you up there," he said, gritting his teeth, "but they sure didn't do you any favors."

"Why don't you and Donald go wrestle each other?" She put her sunglasses back on, looking annoyed. She turned away, but Brian wasn't backing down, and for a second I thought he was going to hit her. A car horn blasted.

"Hey, Brian! Come on, man, let's go!" We all looked up. It was Ben. He was driving a huge, beat-up Bronco with a rebel flag in the back window. The radio blasted Tupac. Ben kind of nodded at me. Acknowledging me, but nothing more. I squinted at him. I was glad we didn't have any dissections coming up.

"Later, faggot." Brian swaggered off toward the behemoth with Donald trotting closely behind him. The engine grunted and they took off. Maria gave them the finger, but it was futile. We went into the trees to retrieve my bike.

"Man," she sighed as we pulled it from a thorn bush. "He really messed it up." I stood the bike upright. The chain had come off, but it wasn't broken. The back tire rim was bent, though. There was no way I could go anywhere on it now.

"I don't know how I'm gonna get it home."

"Worry about that later," Maria said. "Come on. We'll take mine." I limped my bike over to the rack and tried to tie it up with the two broken chain pieces.

"Both of us? Where am I gonna ride, on the handlebars?"

"No. On the back." She led me to the farthest rack. There, chained up like an ordinary bike, was a blue Vespa motor scooter, like something out of *Roman Holiday*. "Cool, innit?"

"I'm downright speechless," I finally said.

"But the beat goes on. Here." She popped open a compartment under the seat and handed me a small, stylish black helmet. "Safety first." I strapped it on and climbed on behind her. She revved the engine until it hummed.

"Hold on to me tight," she commanded. "Don't worry about being fresh."

I slipped my arms loosely around her waist, trying not to go too low or too high. She was warm and smelled a little like lavender and cigarette smoke. We took off faster than I anticipated. Startled, I squeezed her, and she laughed.

"I told you to hold on!" She pulled out into traffic and we sped past the doctors' offices and fast food restaurants, past the retirement home and the hospital. Her hair whipped around my face as we buzzed along. It smelled like almonds. There was a cool smell in the air, too, the smell of the woods, of old trees.

Winter coming on, I guess.

I Didn't Have the Nerve to Say No

Maria was flipping through the two-dollar-shirt racks. "So what is it you like so much about Debbie Harry, anyway?" We'd just spent an hour in Rocksteady, where Maria bought a Françoise Hardy album and Lucas talked me into making a chronological-order exception for *Parallel Lines*. He said it was his favorite Blondie album, and there was a great picture of Debbie on the cover in a white dress, with matching white stilettos and a white armband. She looked like she was about to kick somebody's butt. "I mean, besides the obvious?"

"I dunno. I guess it's just the whole thing. The

music. The band. I like the way they look. I like her style. She's tough, but she's really beautiful, too. I want—" I stopped.

"What?"

I felt lame saying what I almost said. It would've been a dumb thing to say, especially after Brian and those guys.

"What were you gonna say, Johnny?" Maria persisted.

"I was gonna say—" I stopped again. "It's probably going to sound stupid, because she's a girl and everything, but sometimes I wanna be like that. You know, kind of cool and tough but—"

"Beautiful?" she finished.

"I guess so. Yeah. It's just . . . when you're a guy . . . I dunno. It's different." I was blushing. Maria didn't seem to notice. She pulled a purple velveteen scarf from a bin and swept it around her neck. She went to the full-length mirror and posed. I watched her as she pulled her hair away from her face and piled it all on top of her head. She sucked in her cheeks and pouted her lips, then exhaled.

"I wish I looked more like Charlotte Rampling," she said, unwinding the scarf.

"Charlotte Rampling from *Stardust Memories*?" I couldn't believe she'd heard of Charlotte Rampling.

"Yeah. I can't believe you've seen *Stardust Memories*."

"Stranger things have come on cable TV at two in the morning," I told her. "You should get that scarf."

"Really? You think so?"

"Yeah. It's swank."

"All right, then." She draped it over her arm. "In the interest of swankiness."

We walked on through the ladies' section. Two little kids with sticky hands chased past us. Their mom yelled after them.

"You shouldn't let Brian and those guys bother you," Maria said suddenly. "I mean, it sucks, what they did to your bike, but I think they're just playing around. Now they've had their fun and they'll move on."

"I don't know about that." I stopped to look at a pair of black Beatle boots. "That guy Ben's in my biology class. He seems all right. But I don't think Brian likes me and you hanging around together."

"Well, he's just gonna have to get over it." Her

eyes flashed. "I'm sorry he's such an asshole to you, though."

"You don't have to apologize for him."

"I know. He should apologize for himself. Those are cool boots."

"They're ladies'." I started to put them back. "I don't think they'll fit."

"You'll never know till you try 'em on."

"Okay." I untied my Chuck Taylors. "It's just weird, you know? I've never had to deal with guys like them before. There were cliques and stuff in Tampa, but people were pretty much live-and-let-live. I never had any enemies. These guys are, like, living up to every horrible redneck jock cliché—I almost feel embarrassed for them."

"I know. I seriously think they're on steroids. How do those fit?"

"Remarkably well." I took a few steps. "How do I look?"

"Oh, yeah. Those boots were made for walkin'. You gotta buy 'em. If they're cheap enough."

I took them off and looked at the price. "Six bucks."

"Wow."

"What?"

"I just realized. You have really small feet."

"I'm a small guy."

"They're very cute."

"All right. Enough." I was getting mildly annoyed.

"Oh, come on. It's not an insult. That old saying isn't true, anyway."

"How do you know?" I grumbled.

Maria just waggled her eyebrows at me. I tucked the boots under my arm and we walked to the other side of the store.

"Johnny!" Maria grabbed my elbow.

"What?"

"Oh, my gosh, check it out." She pointed to a mannequin in a familiar-looking white dress.

"It's just like—" I didn't finish. The dress was just like the one Debbie wore on the cover of the album I'd just bought.

"The straps have ruffles, but otherwise—"

"It's just like Debbie's." I finished Maria's sentence. "You know—" I stopped, about to say something *really* crazy. I almost—well, it sounded nuts, but I wanted to *wear* that dress. I swallowed hard.

"It's a great dress," Maria said, looking at me

strangely. I wondered if I'd accidentally said what I was thinking out loud. "I think I'm gonna buy it," she announced.

"You are?"

She went up and looked at the price tag, which was hanging in the armpit.

"Ten bucks. It's a steal. C'mere, baby." She started undressing the poor unsuspecting mannequin.

"Don't you think you should ask for some help?" I asked as she pulled the dress over the mannequin's head. "You can't just leave it naked."

"You're absolutely right." Maria grabbed a fur coat from a nearby rack and draped it across the mannequin's shoulders.

"Now she looks like a pimp."

"And all the other mannequins are her bitches. Come on." Maria gathered up the dress and the scarf and me, and we headed to the register.

Atomic

"That was a fast one!" Bug exclaimed, squinting up into the sun.

I'd told Sam I would take her out to the field at Langley and let her shoot off rockets while he went antiquing with Judy. It was fun, actually. Bug set them up and detonated them, or whatever, and they whizzed off into the cloudy sky. Perfect weather for rockets, she assured me. Bug was a smart kid, handy with stuff. She even helped me fix the bike.

"Hey, Bug, wait up," I called out to her. "Sunscreen time." Bug made a face, but she let me slather SPF 45 all over her freckled nose.

"This stinks," Bug complained. "And I have to go retrieve the rocket."

"You know what the real astronauts have for sunscreen?"

"What"

"Gold masks."

"Nuh-uh."

"Yeah-huh. They make the spacesuit masks out of real gold to protect the astronauts from UV rays. And you know the pan your dad makes eggs in so they slide right out?"

"Yeah."

"The stuff that keeps the eggs from sticking to the pan is the same stuff they put on spacesuits so that little pieces of space junk that are flying through the air at a hundred miles an hour just bounce right off the spacemen."

Bug looked at me. Her brow furrowed. "I think that's a load of bull poop," she decided.

"It is not!" That was all I could remember from my trip to the Space Center. "Why would I lie to you?"

"Because you're not very scientific. And you're a *weirdo*!"

"*I'm* a weirdo? *I'm* a weirdo?" I grabbed at Bug, and she squealed and ran. I chased her around the field until I saw Maria standing at the edge of the track, watching. I let Bug go and retrieve her rocket.

"Hey, Johnny," she called out to me. We'd been eating lunch together all week, out behind the bleachers.

"Hi," I said. "What are you doing here?"

"Looking for you. I called your house and your uncle Sam"—you could tell she got a big kick out of saying that—"told me you were out here. He also said to tell you he's back from the antique store and don't forget dinner's at seven."

"Oh. Thanks." I didn't know what else to say. I suddenly felt kind of dumb, hanging out at the school, shooting off rockets with my cousin. Just then, Bug came running up with rocket parts in her hands.

"I found it! All the way past the goalpost!" She made a notation in her rocket notebook, then glanced up at Maria.

"Hi, I'm Maria. I'm a friend of Johnny's."

"Johnny's a weirdo. We're shooting off rockets. You can watch if you want to."

"Okay." Maria smiled. Bug started hooking up a fresh rocket.

"So what's going on?" I asked Maria.

"I was wondering if you wanted to come over and hang out tonight. I have something I want to give you."

"Sounds intriguing."

"Come over around eight?"

"All right."

"Okay, I'll see you then. Bye, Bug."

"Wait! It's countdown!" Bug called to her.

"Look out." I took Maria's hand and pulled her back a few steps, away from the rocket.

"Ten . . . nine . . . eight . . ." Bug started the countdown. Maria's hand was still in mine.

"Five . . . four . . ." Maria was smiling and the wind was blowing her hair and, for a second, she actually did remind me of Charlotte Rampling. She was beautiful.

"Two . . . one—ignition!" Bug hit the button and the rocket blasted off. There was a whooshing noise as it went up. Maria squeezed my hand.

"Wow, that's the highest yet!" Bug exclaimed, running off after it. I turned to look at Maria, and, before I knew what was happening, she kissed me on the lips.

"Wow," I whispered.

"See you tonight, weirdo." She smiled and jogged off.

"This might be a little too . . . heavy for you," Maria explained as she put the record on the turntable. We'd been playing records for hours. "But to me she's just . . ." She shook her head. "I mean, I know every note of this album. It's like my Bible." She lowered the needle and sat down next to me on the bed. There was a crackle, and a few spare piano notes.

"Jesus died for somebody's sins, but not mine," a throaty voice announced from the speakers.

"That's some Bible," I said.

"Shh." Maria put her hand on mine. I looked at the album cover. Black-and-white, the same picture that was on a postcard taped up next to Maria's bed. I thought it was some French movie star from one of those movies like *Jules and Jim,* but it turns out it was Patti Smith. She kind of looked like Maria herself, thin, and with dark, messy hair. She was stylish like Maria, too—posed in a white shirt with a black jacket slung over her shoulder like Frank Sinatra or something.

"You like it so far?" Maria asked after the first couple of songs.

"Yeah, it's pretty . . . intense."

"The next one's really amazing." She lay down on the bed. "Come here." I lay down next to her, not sure how close I should get. We faced each other while the next song unraveled. It was like a poem about this kid seeing UFOs in a field. Maria held my hands, but I was afraid to make a move. Afraid to scare her away. Then she started kissing me. Little kisses on my nose and eyes, and then my lips. I started to lose track of the music.

"Hang on." She got up and flipped the record, then came back to her place on the bed. The songs were fast, slow, fast—I wasn't really paying attention. There was just a voice, and Maria, letting me touch her, and hold her, and kiss her, and she kissed back, and when it was all over we were both lying there on the bed with all our clothes on, hanging on to each other with sweaty hands. I felt like I'd been somewhere, like I'd been gone for a long time and I'd been running the whole way. My lips felt numb. I was shaking a little. It was the most drunk I'd been since I'd stopped drinking.

The needle clicked back over to its starting point, and the room was quiet. I wasn't sure what to do next. I didn't want to break the spell. Maria sat up first. I sat up next to her on the edge of the bed. She smoothed her hair and lit a cigarette.

"Did you like it?" Her voice was soft. I nodded. She was quiet. She took another drag and pushed her hair behind her ear.

"My mom is like completely"—she exhaled— "obsessed with Patti Smith. They were both from New Jersey and they both lived in New York at the same time. She gave me that jacket last Christmas," Maria pointed at the black blazer she wore when-ever she wasn't in her school uniform, hanging up on her closet door. "She said she got it from this woman who lived at the Chelsea Hotel the same time as Patti, back in the seventies. The woman said Patti left it behind when she moved, and it's the same jacket from the album cover." I looked at the picture. They did look awfully similar, but then, a lot of black jackets look alike.

"I know she was probably lying. I mean, the woman lied to my mom. Or my mom lied to me. But I kind of like to pretend it's true, anyway. Kinda stupid, right?" I didn't know what to say, so I held her hand while she finished her cigarette and stubbed it out in a Coke can by her bed.

"It's not stupid," I said finally. She just smiled at me.

"You wanna see what I got you?" She stood up. The spell was gone.

"Sure."

She turned on the lamp, and I blinked, feeling my pupils stretch. "You didn't have to get me anything."

"Well, it's not exactly a surprise." She opened her closet door. "But here it is. New and improved!"

It was the dress. The *Parallel Lines* dress.

"I took some of the fabric off the straps—you can use it for an armband. And I let the hem out a little for you."

"But, why, for me?" I stammered.

"You can be tough and beautiful, just like Debbie." She smiled. "Here. Try it on."

"But, Maria." I tried to laugh. "It's a *dress*." I felt

like I was trying to sober up. I mean, wearing eye-liner was one thing. Even Robert Smith wore lipstick. But this was a woman's dress!

"I'm well aware." She gave me a sly smile and started unbuttoning my shirt. I yanked myself away.

"What the hell are you doing? Are you making fun of me or something? Knock it off!"

She backed away. "I'm sorry. I thought—I thought you'd like it. I thought it would be fun. You could pretend—I mean, you said you wanted to be like—" She stopped. "I'm sorry, Johnny." She put the dress back on its hanger and sat down on the bed.

This was all coming apart. How did I lose control? What was going on? I couldn't think. One minute I had my hand up her shirt, the next minute she was trying to get me to put on a dress. A dress that I secretly sort of wanted to put on. What kind of kinky shit was this?

I looked back at her. She was just sitting on the bed, reading the back of the album cover. I wanted to believe she was honest, that she wasn't making fun of me. That she was on my side. But she was real. And that's the problem with real people. They can form opinions about you, just like you form opinions about them. Unlike posters, or album covers, or voices on records that always say the same thing whenever you put them on. Real people can feel free to voice their contrary opinions any damn time they please.

My face was hot. I took off my shirt. My Beatle boots. My socks. I hesitated a second, then took off my pants. I could see in the mirror that Maria was watching me, but I kept telling myself I didn't care. I wanted to tell her something—why did I always feel like that? Like I wanted her to come to me and say "What is it?" and I could lay it all on her? That was all I needed her to say.

I pulled the dress off the hanger. My hands were shaking. What was so scary about putting on a girl's dress? Debbie's dress? Even though I knew it really wasn't, I could almost believe it really was hers.

I unzipped the dress and slipped it on over my head. The fabric was light and silky and slid easily down around my body. The top was a little loose, obviously, but the rest was a perfect fit.

"Hold still." Maria was standing behind me now. "Let me zip you up." I could feel her knuckle grazing my spine as she pulled the zipper all the way up.

The fabric tightened around me, hugging my ribs. I turned and faced her. I didn't feel so tough. What was it I wanted to tell her? That she was beautiful? That even though we'd just met I already loved her? That I missed my mother, and my father, too? That I wanted to be somewhere else all the time, but I didn't know where or how to get there?

"Johnny." She put her hand on my cheek. "What's the matter?"

I started to cry. It was awful. I just couldn't stop crying. But she didn't laugh. Even though my face was wet and snotty, she pulled me toward her and hugged me. I cried into her shirt, gasping for each soggy breath. She smoothed back my hair and kissed me on the forehead.

"I'm sorry." My voice was thick. "I'm sorry. I'm just being stupid. I'm crazy. I don't know."

"You're beautiful. You're just so beautiful. There's nothing to be sorry about." She turned me around to see my reflection in the mirror. "That's all you have to do. Just be beautiful."

Will Anything Happen?

I'd been assigned to a counselor at school, Mr. Briggs. Monday was my first meeting with him, and I felt a little weird about it. But I was feeling a little weird about a lot of things all of a sudden.

"So, how's things, John?" Briggs sat back in his chair, relaxed. He seemed like the classic guidance counselor, trying to be hip with the kids. He even had blond highlights in his hair.

"Not bad. It's Johnny, by the way."

"Johnny. Right, sorry." He made a note on a clipboard in his lap. He read over my file. "So. Been drinking lately?" Wow, right to the point.

"No."

"And how's that working out for you?"

"I fall down a lot less."

He chuckled and grabbed a handful of cashews from a bowl on his desk. "Cashew?" he offered.

"No, thanks. You know, you don't have to try to impress me with how cool and casual you are, or whatever."

"I'm not out to impress you, John. I'm out to stuff myself silly with cashews, and if I can make you comfortable in the meantime, that's just extra. Now, back to your drinking problem."

"Well . . ." This was a little weird. He honestly didn't seem to give a damn. "I just haven't been drinking. I've been keeping it on the straight and narrow. I don't know what else to tell you."

"How d'you manage it?"

"Manage what?"

"I mean, I don't even have the willpower to make myself stop eating these cashews. How do you keep yourself from drinking?"

"I think about girls," I said bluntly. He laughed.

"That's new. Girls in general or one girl in particular?" I thought of Debbie. And Maria.

"One or two in particular."

"Right." He nodded and popped another cashew. "You came to us from Florida, I see. How do you like it here?"

"It blows."

"Don't hold back, John."

"Sorry. It's just different. It's so . . . claustrophobic up here. I mean, not just the landscape. It's like everybody's been here forever. They all know each other and each other's parents. It's weird. People were more laid-back in Florida. Everybody was just . . . cool, you know? I had a lot of friends; we all hung out and partied. It didn't matter if your parents had money or whatever. I guess it's just a different vibe."

"You would've had to give up the party lifestyle anyway, though. Correct?"

"Yeah, I guess."

"So how's the school treating you?"

"Badly," I said, and he smirked. "It doesn't matter, though. I think high school is just supposed to suck."

"Not necessarily. What's so awful about it?"

I thought about Brian Quinn and his buddies. And thought that they'd probably kick my ass for real if I ratted them out. "Oh, you know, the usual," I told him, nonchalant.

"Crap food, crap teachers, bigger guys beating you up after school?" He neatly arched an eyebrow at me.

"Something like that, yeah." I breathed tightly. He looked at me coolly. I cleared my throat and glared back at him.

"How did you end up here, John?"

"I came up the stairs and took a left at the nurse's station."

"Wiseass." He rolled his eyes. "I mean how'd you end up in this school? In this state?" Did he mean how did I end up in South Carolina or my mental state? I was afraid to ask.

"Doesn't it say why in your notes? I thought you doctors kept up with each other."

"I'm not a doctor. I'm a counselor. And, yes, it does say. But I want to hear it from you."

"I had a drinking problem. And my mother sent me away."

"And how do you feel about that?"

"I hate it."

"What do you hate? Your mother? The school?"

"Everything! I hate everything about it!" I blew up. "I hate that I took care of everything for her and she just sent me away! I hate that I became—" For a second, I remembered that less than forty-eight hours ago I was standing in Maria's bedroom in a ladies' dress.

"That you became what?"

"That I became somebody she couldn't handle."

He didn't have anything to say to that, at first.

"Do you hate your mother?" he asked. I thought about it for a moment.

"No. Well . . . she definitely pisses me off sometimes, and I wish she hadn't sent me away. I do feel like I hate her, sometimes. But she's my mom. I guess I love her, deep down."

He looked at me for a long time. "You know that it's not your fault that she couldn't handle your problems."

"Yeah, I know."

"All right, then, good." He clapped his hands together and brushed salt off them. "Now, can I ask you about your dad?"

"It's a free country." I shrugged.

"Your father passed away, correct?"

"Yeah. Correct."

"How did he die?" Briggs looked at me, all serious. I shifted in my seat.

"Look, can't you just read all this stuff in my file?"

"Yes, but I thought I'd give you a chance to tell your side of it. If it's still too sensitive an issue for you, by all means—"

"It's not *sensitive.*" I felt annoyed all over again. "He got in a car accident and died. It's typical and stupid. I was twelve. Boo hoo. I'm over it now."

"Are you?" He cocked his head at me. Of course I wasn't, but somehow I felt bullied into talking about the whole thing. I felt defensive. But I wanted to talk about it, all of a sudden. Just to prove that I could.

"I dunno," I sighed. "Sometimes I think about him all the time. Sometimes I go for days—I almost forget it happened. Being up here, sometimes it's easier, because nothing reminds me of him. He was away all the time, anyway. Mostly it's like he's still gone on a business trip."

"The uncle you live with now is your father's brother, correct?"

"Yeah."

"And how do you two get along?"

"Fine. He's a cool guy. He's—it's like he talks to everybody the same, you know? It doesn't matter how old you are. He's not one of those guys who's always trying to teach you a lesson or something."

"Mm-hmm." Briggs scratched a note on his pad. "Does he remind you of your father?"

"No."

"What was he like?"

"My dad? He was . . ." I clicked through memories of my dad like a slideshow. What was he like? He didn't have hobbies. He wasn't one of those dads who was into golf, or fishing, or cars. He didn't have a lot of *things.* Personal effects. What kind of guy was he? I tried to think of somebody to compare him to. Mr. Brady. Cliff Huxtable. Ward Cleaver. John Goodman on *Roseanne.* He wasn't like any of those guys.

"My dad wasn't around too much. When he was around, he didn't say much. I remember him and my mom at the dinner table. . . . She did most of the talking. I think he loved her, though. When he came in she used to kind of . . . take him in her arms and hold him for a really long time." I felt embarrassed all of a sudden. This probably wasn't the kind of stuff Briggs wanted to know.

"He wasn't ever mean to me. He drank a good bit, but we didn't fight or anything. He taught me how to play soccer when I was little. It's, uh . . ." Thinking about it, I realized that my dad didn't have a whole heck of a lot of personality. "He was kind of quiet. And his clothes never fit."

"His clothes never fit?"

"No. He dressed nice. I remember mom always ironing his work shirts and taking his suits to the dry cleaners. But they never fit right. His watch didn't even fit. It was one of those with the stretchy metal bands. I could never figure out why he didn't get it fixed, or get his pants hemmed." My mom always hemmed my pants because I was so small. But my dad was always stepping on his cuffs. I thought about all those nights, sitting in front of the TV. The smoke curling out of the cigarette between his fingers. The way he stared into the dark, just sitting there.

"Are you mad at your father, Johnny?"

"No. I think I was at first, but not anymore."

"You miss him?"

"I guess. Yeah." It was like missing a shadow or a gap in your teeth. I missed missing him. "Sometimes I think I didn't even get to know him. Sometimes I think I'm still waiting for him to come home."

Briggs just looked at me for a while, then he stood up.

"I think that's enough for today, don't you?"

"All right." I grabbed my bag. I felt like I was waking up from a trance.

"Here's my card, if you need to talk outside of school hours." He handed me a white card with his name in black letters, his phone number beneath. "See you around, John." We shook hands, and I went off to find Maria.

"So how was it?" We were sitting under the bleachers.

"Fine. He asked if I was drinking and if I hated my mother. Then I had to talk about my dad."

"Typical." She took a drag from her cigarette. "Are you okay?"

"Yeah. I'm sorry I spazzed out about the—the dress thing the other night." My words came out in a rush. "I guess I was having sort of a weird time."

"It's okay." She put her hand on mine. I laced my fingers through hers. "It was a heavy night. I'm glad you came over."

"I'm glad you invited me."

"Hey, ladies."

Maria and I both turned around. Brian Quinn was standing there with Donald and Ben.

"Oh, Christ," Maria muttered. "What do you guys want?"

"We wanna smoke in peace," Brian announced.

"Without no faggots around," Donald chimed in.

"Yeah, this is a fag-free zone," Brian added.

I looked at Ben, waiting for him to chime in. He just stood there, his fists in his pockets. There was no expression on his face, but he was blushing.

"All right, I get the point." I got up. Maria was still sitting there. "Let's go."

"No, I'm finishing my cigarette," she announced. She had about half to go. Brian walked over.

"You heard her—get lost."

"Oh, give me a break," I said suddenly. "What do you know about her?"

"I know plenty more than you ever will," Brian challenged.

"Oh, yeah?" I couldn't believe I was getting into this. "Then . . . who's her favorite Beatle?"

"Her favorite *Beatle*? Who fucking cares? Nobody listens to that old shit no more."

"*We* do." Maria gave me a secretive little smile, like we were members of an exclusive club.

"You said you know more about her than I do." I shrugged at him, feeling suddenly more assured. "Prove it."

"All right, it's John Lennon," he said confidently.

"Wrong. It's George."

"Bullshit," he scoffed. "Maria, who's your favorite goddamn Beatle?"

"George Harrison," she deadpanned. Ben chuckled. Brian shot him a death look.

"Man, fuck this shit. Gimme a cigarette, Maria."

"No," she said.

"Damn. You been hanging around fags too long. Donnie, gimme a smoke." Donald obliged, handing Brian a Camel. He lit it with a shiny Zippo.

"All right." He exhaled smoke in my direction. "I'm gonna count to ten and you better get lost. Ten . . . nine . . ."

"Ooh, he can count backward." Maria stood up, brushing the dust from her skirt.

"Eight . . . seven . . . six . . ."

"Monkeys *can* be taught," she continued.

"Come on, man," Ben muttered to Brian. "Just let 'em go. You get in trouble, you're gonna get suspended off the team."

"Oops, time's up." Brian grabbed me suddenly by the collar and pushed me backward.

"Get your hands off him!" Maria yelled. I didn't have time to react. He kept pushing until finally I lost my footing and landed with a hard thud on my rear end. Maria ran to me and crouched down.

"Ow." My hand stung. I looked down and saw blood—I'd tried to catch myself and hit a rock.

"Brian, you dumbass!" She shoved him, but he barely moved. "Why do you have to be such a jerk all the time?"

"Why do you have to hang around with pussy queers?"

Maria turned on her heel and groaned, exasperated.

"You didn't used to be like this, Brian." She helped me to my feet. "Come on, Johnny."

We walked off in silence. I guess Brian couldn't think of any more insults.

A few minutes later, in the boys' bathroom, Maria was back to playing nurse, cleaning my wound with a soapy paper towel.

"That stings!" I drew back my hand. She pulled it toward her and blew lightly on it.

"How's that?"

"Now it just tickles." She stopped and looked at me. She wiped a smudge of dirt off my face.

"Those guys piss me off so much, I don't know what to do." She shook her head. "I don't know how you can stay so calm."

"They're clowns." I shrugged. "I mean, they piss me off, too, but I'm trying not to take it too personally anymore. They're just narrow-minded bullies."

"I mean, you're not even *gay*," she muttered.

"He didn't count all the way down, either. They aren't really going by the rules."

"I don't think he knew what came before six."

She laughed. "Look at this—you're the one getting pushed around, and now you're comforting *me*."

"Somebody's gotta wear the pants around here," I said. "And my dress is at the cleaners." She laughed again. It was possibly the greatest sound in the world.

"That reminds me . . . listen, don't hate me for this, it's kind of far out—"

"What is it?"

"Well, this may be crazy . . ."

"We'll never know if you don't say it."

"Sorry." She smiled. "It's just, well, my grand-mother lives in Atlanta, right? Well, um, there's this club there I know of, and they're having this big—well, they're having this big drag contest." She said the last part quickly, like it was all one word.

"By drag I assume you don't mean auto racing."

"No," she replied. "It's called Night of a Thousand Divas. It's kind of famous. And it's in two weeks, so you'd have to get a routine together pretty fast. But I thought maybe you could get a wig and— I mean, the prize money is seven hundred dollars."

"Wow." A drag contest. "You're right. It's crazy."

I looked at her—she was clearly excited. "Why do you care, anyway?"

"What—what do you mean? Why do I care about you?"

"Yeah. Why do you care so much about me putting on this dress? What's in it for you?"

"It's fun." She looked down at my hand and wiped off imaginary dirt. "And I haven't had any fun around here in a long time."

"Sometimes I wonder if you're having fun or making fun."

"Having. Definitely having." She paused. "Johnny, I would never put this much time and effort into making fun of you. I'm too lazy." She smiled. "I just think—you know, I get why you're so into the whole Blondie thing, and you said you wanted to be like Debbie, and this is a way you can be." The bell rang.

"It's just an idea." She shrugged. "We'd better go."

I followed her out, remembering Debbie's dress and Maria's hands on my back as the zipper went up. Seven hundred dollars would buy an awful lot of records.

"I'll think about it," I told her as we went to class.

Man Overboard

I was just riding around after school. I told Maria I had to be home early to look after Bug, but it wasn't true. After all that talk about my dad with Mr. Briggs and the episode with Brian and the drag contest, I was feeling unsettled. I tried to call Terry, but that was a bust.

"Hello?" As soon as he picked up the phone, I could hear loud music and a girl's voice in the background.

"Hey, Terry, it's me."

"Who?"

"It's Johnny."

"Oh, hey, man. How's South Dakota?"

"South Car—uh, it's great. Listen, you got a minute?"

"Sure. What's up?"

"Well, it's kinda weird. I met this girl, and she's really great. But . . . " I didn't even know how to get into it. "She bought this dress and she invited me over—"

"What? She got undressed and did what? Are you gettin' laid?"

"No, no, not undressed." I sighed. This was frustrating. "She's got this boyfriend who's really got it in for me. Ex-boyfriend. He's on the wrestling team—"

"Her boyfriend wants to do *what* to you? Hang on." He put his hand over the receiver, but I could hear him anyway. "Steph! Tell them to turn that damn— Hey! I don't care who she is! I'm on the phone! I'm on the— Hey! Cut it out!" There were muffled sounds, more music and crashing, and then Terry came back on the line.

"Hey, listen, Johnny, can you call me back later on tonight? We've got some people over and it's getting kinda crazy."

"Yeah, okay." I didn't want to call him back.

"Right on. Have fun with them cows, cowboy!"

I hung up the phone and went downstairs. Judy had just gotten there with Bug, who looked very cranky. Judy was making her a snack.

"Oh, hi, Johnny. You want an apple with peanut butter on it?" Judy asked.

"No, thanks. Is Sam around?" I shoved my hands in my pockets so they wouldn't see my scraped palms.

"He's still at work, but he'll be back soon. I'm sure he wouldn't mind you calling him."

"No, that's okay. It's not urgent. I just had a question for him."

"Okay. Well, we're getting ready to work on Bug's costume for the Christmas pageant! Right, Bug?"

"Yeah." Bug wasn't too enthused, and, for the first time, I could see why she didn't like Judy. Bug didn't like being talked down to. Judy had that sort of put-on enthusiasm, like when you talk to a three-year-old. One thing I knew about Bug, she didn't want to be treated like a little kid.

"I'm gonna run an errand. I'll be right back." I grabbed my house keys and headed for the garage. Bug followed me.

"Hey, Johnny," she whispered, "later on tonight, will you help me with my Christmas pageant costume?"

"Yeah. But what about Judy? Isn't she helping you?" I lowered my own voice.

"She wants me to be Betsy Ross. And I don't want to."

"Betsy Ross? What does she have to do with Christmas?"

"It's before the Christmas part. We all have to dress as an American hero and walk out and say a speech about why they're our hero. I wanna be Sally Ride, but Judy says the costume's too hard to make. But you know about space stuff, and she doesn't. Sally Ride was the first American woman in space."

"I know." I looked at the expression on Bug's face. She was dead serious.

"What about your mom?"

"She wanted me to be Princess Di."

"Princess Di? She's British."

"I know. Will you help me make a Sally Ride costume?"

"Well . . ." What did I know about making a space suit? Maria was good at sewing—I could ask her for tips. How hard could it be? "Sure. We can do it," I told her.

"Okay. Good. Just make sure Judy doesn't find out."

"Why don't you just tell her that now I'm helping you instead?"

"I asked her in the beginning if you could help us, but she said you're a boy and you can't sew," Bug whispered. "Besides, if I tell her she doesn't know enough about space, she'll feel bad."

The kid killed me.

"Okay. We'll work on it tonight, after dinner." I got on my bike, and Bug went back in the house, smiling.

I found myself heading toward Rocksteady Records. I wanted to see Maria, but I felt like I needed to talk to a *guy*, someone who wouldn't sway me with the overwhelming power of her almond-smelling hair.

"Johnny Ace, back for more?" Lucas called out as I walked in. He was playing some Chuck Berry–sounding garage band.

"I dunno. Thought I'd browse." I didn't have a dollar in my pocket. "So, uh, what's new with you?"

"Slow day." He spritzed a paper towel with some clear solution from a spray bottle and wiped it carefully around a dusty record sitting on the counter in front of him. "Where's your girlfriend?"

"I felt like being by myself for a little bit." I shrugged. "I guess I just wasn't in a girl mood. Is that a jerk thing to say?"

"Maybe if you say it to a girl. Everything okay with Maria?"

"Yeah. Why wouldn't it be?"

"I dunno, man." He slipped the clean record back into its sleeve and started on another one. "Forget it, it's none of my business."

"No, say what you're going to say." Somehow I knew this would be ugly. I braced myself for whatever horrible thing Lucas was about to tell me.

"Look, man, I don't like to gossip. I'm just tryin' to look out for you, right? A couple of years ago, I was at this party, and that chick, Maria, comes in with a bunch of guys. And they were all drunk and high."

"Maria doesn't even drink," I interrupted.

"Well, she was drinking that night. I ended up talking to her for a while—" He stopped and looked at me. If Lucas was about to tell me he slept with her, I thought I might fall flat on the floor and never get up.

"And then one of the guys she came with started trippin', throwing beer bottles at people, saying all this crazy paranoid shit. Somebody said they were gonna call the cops, so me and her went and hid in the bathroom. She was freaking out and I tried to bring her down a little, you know. Then she starts telling me her life story, and, man, if it wasn't the saddest thing I ever heard. Her dad's some cop or something who barely says a word to her. Her mom bailed on them and never tries to contact her or see her or anything. She has to take care of the house and her dad. She told me she never ate or slept anymore, she just stayed up all night and went out with these guys, but she didn't even like them. She said she was tired of it and she just wanted to split, but, you know, the way she said it, I dunno if she meant get outta town or, you know—" Lucas's voice was quiet. I leaned hard against the counter. I felt like I was going to cry.

"I didn't know what to do. She was at the end of her rope. You just wanted to give this chick some hot soup and put her to bed, you know? But I . . . I went to give her a hug, you know? Just a hug, and it was like she couldn't believe it. She flinched like I was gonna hit her. And after I hugged her, she looked at me like I was some kinda alien. She said nobody had *fucking hugged* her in forever, and she just started bawling. It was the saddest damn thing I ever saw. I guess after that she went away—or got sent away—for a while."

"Jesus," I rasped. My throat felt like sandpaper.

"I don't mean to be talking shit about her, you know, since she's your girl, and all. I mean, she looks a lot better now, too, like she's straightened out in her own head. At least she looks like she's eating. But, you know, be careful with that one, man. She's had a rough time."

"Yeah." I nodded, wondering why I thought coming here would make me feel better. Lucas went back to cleaning records. I didn't even feel like browsing. "Well, I guess I better go."

"All right. Hang tough, Johnny Ace."

I waved and walked out into the sunset. The trees were dark, woven tight against the violet sky. I thought about Maria being alone, her dad working all the time and her mom too broke to visit. I thought about Christmas coming up. Seven hundred dollars could buy a plane ticket to New York, couldn't it?

The next day, Maria and I were at the public library, down in the musty-smelling basement. Bound in big brown-leather books were old issues of *Rolling Stone* magazine that hadn't seen the light of day in at least a decade, if not two. We pulled out 1975–1982 and perched side by side on rubber-topped stepstools, turning the brittle pages. Maria thought I would get inspired about the drag show if I saw enough pictures of Debbie Harry.

"Look, here's another one." Maria put one of the books in my lap, pointing to a black-and-white picture with the caption *Blondie on stage at CBGB, 1978.* She looked ferocious, in a short dress, torn fishnets, and stiletto boots.

"What's CBGB?"

"It's a club in New York. I went one time—my mom's boyfriend played there with his band. It's this totally dingy little bar, but everybody cool started at CBGB. Blondie, the Ramones, Patti Smith, Talking

Heads. It's, like, half the size of the Village Green. You wouldn't believe it. Maybe I'll take you there someday."

"That would be cool." How on earth would Maria and I ever make it to New York? My mom would kill me. If we didn't get killed by some insane mugger or something first.

"But first things first. Let's go to Atlanta. It'll be so much fun, I promise."

"I don't know."

"Are you afraid those guys at school will find out? I won't tell. And so what if they do? It's like a big costume party."

"It's not just that." I looked at the picture of Debbie. Smoothed the fifteen-year-old page beneath my palm. "I just don't think I could . . . *be* like that."

"What do you mean? You've got the dress. We get you a wig, some shoes—"

"It's not just the costume. It's just . . . I'm not strong enough or cool enough or brave enough or anything. I'm just . . . myself."

"Johnny." Maria looked at me seriously. "You're thinking. Stop it."

"Stop thinking?"

"I'm serious. Look at this woman." She pointed to the picture. "I've been to CBGB. It takes a lot of attitude to get up on that stage. And if you start thinking, 'Oh, I'm not cool, I'm not strong,' whatever, then you'll never be able to do it. You just put on your dress and your high heels and you get out there and you kick some ass!"

I laughed.

"You think we should go to Atlanta, huh?"

"Hey, at least it's a different town. If you fail miserably, you won't know anyone in the audience. It'll be our little secret. The day you sucked at dressing up like Debbie Harry."

She was right. I couldn't stop thinking. I was thinking about that night in her room, putting on the dress. I was thinking about Lucas and what he'd said about Maria being so alone. I looked down at the picture again. At Debbie, taking no prisoners in her stiletto boots.

"You'll have to teach me how to walk in heels," I said.

Walk Like Me

"You're good at that." Maria watched as I traced my eyes with a black kohl pencil in the mirror. It was Saturday. We'd spent the morning working on Bug's costume, until she and Uncle Sam left for the planetarium. We spent the afternoon working on mine.

"Years of dutiful study of old Cure videos." I touched up my lipstick and turned to face her.

"Wow." She looked really surprised. "You're really beautiful."

"All right." I was blushing. "Where's my hair?"

She reached for the bag she'd brought with her. Inside was a short, platinum-blond wig. Maria tucked my hair into a nylon cap and wiggled the wig onto my head.

"It's tight," I complained.

"It's supposed to be. That way your hair won't fall off when you're shakin' your ass. Okay, turn around."

I faced the mirror. "It's kind of . . ."

"Fake-looking, isn't it? Don't worry, we can give it a little tousle. Stand up, let's see how you move."

It was my first time in stilettos. They weren't exactly the best. We'd spent all our money on the wig and makeup and didn't have much left over. I had the dress on and one of Maria's bras—stuffed— underneath. I felt taller than usual and highly unstable. The girls in the Ramonas had it lucky. All they needed to dress up was jeans and sneakers.

"Looking good. How do you feel?"

"Like I'm going to fall over."

"Walk around, get the feel of the heels." I walked. Maria turned up the stereo—it was Debbie singing "Pretty Baby." I walked back and forth, getting a little more confident with each step.

"All right now," she interrupted. I stopped. "Come on, show me some moves or something."

"What do you mean, moves?"

"I thought you've been practicing!"

"Yeah, lip-synching! I didn't know I had to dance!"

"Johnny." Maria sighed and got up off the bed. "This girl Shawna that I knew at the strip club used to say, 'You don't have to be a Rockette, just learn how to use what you've got.' You know, swing your hips a little, get in the groove."

This was embarrassing. I wanted to sweep her up like Al Pacino in that movie, but I was no Al Pacino. And I was wearing stiletto heels. I tried to move, but it was stiff. I was never getting Maria to New York like this.

"Okay, square one." She stood in front of me, snapping her fingers. "Just feel the beat." We started to move. My ankles wobbled. This wasn't exactly Goth night at the Tower.

"Johnny, come on! Loosen up!" She grabbed my arms and swung them violently. I swayed like a noodle. "That's it! Watusi! Just go loose! *Release your inner Debbie!*" That was it. We collapsed on the bed laughing.

"Excuse me, Johnny?" Uncle Sam stood in the

bedroom doorway. Maria and I both jumped to our feet. My wig slid to one side. Sam's brow furrowed. I yanked the wig the rest of the way off.

"Ah, well, I just wanted to let you know that we're back and—ah, dinner's in an hour." He nodded at Maria. "You're welcome to stay."

"Okay, thanks. Thank you. Sir." Maria's voice sounded high.

I crossed my arms awkwardly in front of my chest as he closed the door. He opened it back up again as soon as it shut.

"Johnny, could I talk to you for a minute in the hallway?"

Maria took the needle off the record as I wobbled out into the hall. Uncle Sam closed the door behind us.

"Um, John, I don't want to seem—ah, insensitive." He spoke carefully, staring down at his hands. "However—"

"You wanna know why I'm wearing a dress," I guessed.

"For starters."

"All right. Well." I cleared my throat. Where did I begin? With Maria and her mother? With Debbie?

"See, it's like—um . . . okay, you know how, sometimes, football players take ballet?"

"It's my fault, Mr. McKenzie." Maria burst out of the room. Uncle Sam just looked at her. "I'm Maria, we spoke on the phone the other day. Anyway, I— dared Johnny to put on a dress."

"No, she didn't—"

"Yes, I did—"

"No, really—"

Uncle Sam was looking from one of us to the other. "Maria, I appreciate you trying to stick up for John. But he's not in trouble. I just wanted to say"— his eyes fell on me—"that if you're having some kind of . . . issues with your . . . ah, your sexuality, you can feel free to come to me, and we'll discuss them. Ah . . . are you—are you gay, John?" He sounded like a librarian asking me to hand in my overdue books.

"No, sir, I don't believe so."

"Good. That's great." He checked himself quickly. "Of course, it's fine if you are—you're free to practice whatever form of—"

"Thanks, I know." I stopped him.

"All right, then." He put his hand on my shoulder. "Just, ah, be careful in those heels."

. . .

Later that night, I went downstairs to get a drink of water. My feet were killing me.

"You're up late." It was Sam. I jumped a mile.

"I was just going to bed."

"Didn't mean to scare you." Uncle Sam took a beer out of the fridge. "You mind?"

"Just because I can't doesn't mean you can't either." I filled my water glass. All through dinner, we'd both been pretty quiet. But now I had a weird feeling he was going to want to discuss things with me "man to man."

"You mind sitting up and talking a bit?" He went to the table. "I know that you've got school tomorrow."

"It's not that late." I sat down across from him. I suddenly felt nervous. He'd kept a six-pack in the back of the fridge ever since I got there, but it was the first time I'd actually seen him drink. I figured maybe it was a test for me or something. Or maybe he was going to get drunk and beat the hell out of me for wearing that dress.

"Do you think Bug would have a hard time if I asked Judy to move in with me?"

That wasn't what I was expecting. "I dunno. You could ask her."

"I know." He sighed. "It's just—she's not too crazy about Roger. I think she likes Judy a little more now, but I don't want to make both her homes uncomfortable."

"Are you and Judy getting married?"

"I guess that's what I should do, shouldn't I? Make an honest woman out of her." Sam smiled and stared off into the corner. "Sometimes I think that's what I like about seeing Judy. Having to sneak off with her. It's kinda like being a teenager again, but instead of your parents catching you making out, it's your kid you gotta worry about."

"Yeah," I mumbled. I didn't really want to hear about my uncle's sex life. But I guess this was what men talk about. I felt like I should put on a suit jacket.

"Well . . . I guess we'll cross that bridge when we come to it. Really, I was . . . well, I was thinking about your dad. I don't know . . . maybe you don't want to talk about it. . . ." He swigged at the beer.

I shrugged. I was never in the mood to talk about my dad. Sometimes it seemed like everybody wanted me to spill my guts every five minutes—Mr. Briggs, Maria, now Uncle Sam. Sometimes I just got tired of talking about it.

"I guess it's just . . . with you around, I've been thinking about him a lot. You really remind me of him. Your mom probably tells you that all the time. Maybe she doesn't. It's not so much the way you look . . . I mean, you're small, like he was."

"Thanks." I grimaced.

"I didn't mean it in a bad way. Anyway, it's more like . . . mannerisms. You're like he was when he was young. Sorta . . . artistic."

"Artistic?" I didn't think of myself as artistic. Heck, I couldn't draw a straight line.

"Yeah, you know, he was into music the way you are. The place we grew up—it was even smaller than this town—people gave him such a hard time because he had long hair. It seems silly now, the way kids dress. His hair wasn't that much longer than mine is. I guess people just make their own . . . I don't know. . . ."

"Yeah," I said lamely. I had no idea what he was talking about. But I suddenly realized that Sam didn't expect *me* to talk about my dad. He wanted to talk. It was a strange thought. It never occurred to me that anybody missed him but my mom and me. And nobody had ever really told me what he was like when he was young.

"Sometimes we didn't get along. Our parents always compared us. They wanted him to be like me and not cause any trouble, and all along I just wanted to be like him. It always seemed like he was having so much fun. He sure got all the girls. He went off to England, and when he came back—" Sam shook his head. "It was so exotic. It was like he might as well have been a sheik."

My dad? A sheik?

"He didn't seem like much of a sheik to me."

"I guess not." Sam laughed and took another drink. "He was pretty well settled by the time you came around. We had a little falling out over it, actually. When he married your mom . . ." He sighed and swigged the beer again. "Look, I like your mom. I guess at the time it just seemed like she wanted him to be something he wasn't. But he said she inspired him. They really seemed to love each other. He cut his hair, got a job, the whole bit."

"The whole bit, huh?" That explained a lot, once

I thought about it. He was a long-haired hippy sheik, and Mom made him do a complete 180. No wonder he was gone so much.

"I miss the hell outta him, Johnny. Even if we didn't always get along. He was my brother." Uncle Sam sounded all choked, and when I looked at him, he was just staring off into the corner again, his jaw clenched tight. I sat there for a while longer, until he finished his beer.

"I better get to bed." I finally stood up. I wasn't sure what else to do.

"Yeah, I reckon it's getting late, huh?" Sam got up and tossed his bottle in the recycling bin. "Thanks for letting me talk."

"Sure, no problem."

"I know you didn't want to move here, Johnny, but I'm glad you're here. I hope it hasn't been all bad."

I thought about Brian and his friends. I thought about my mom, and not being able to talk to Terry anymore. And then I thought about Lucas, and the record shop, and the Village Green. I thought about Maria.

"It's not so bad," I decided. "It's not so bad at all."

Heart of Glass

The night before the show, I took the phone into my room and closed the door. Sam and Judy were downstairs, watching some lame movie about a lawyer trying to solve a murder plot or something. I wasn't into it, and I could tell Uncle Sam was doing his best just to stay awake. I snuck off to call Maria for a pep talk.

"What's up?" I could hear her turning her stereo down. "You're not getting cold feet, are you?"

"No, I've got *sore* feet. I've been practicing in the heels." Truthfully, my feet were pretty cold. I had been practicing, but now I was careful to lock the door. All I needed was for Bug to walk in and ask why I was wearing ladies' shoes. "So, uh, how far is it to Atlanta?"

"It's about a two-and-a-half-hour drive. If we don't hit traffic. But we're not driving in at rush hour, so we're cool."

"Oh. You got your dad's truck?"

"Yeah. He was cool. I just told him I had to drive a friend of mine down to Atlanta for a drag show. He's into it."

"Seriously?"

"No!" She laughed. "I told him that this girl at school invited me on a camping trip. His friend's taking him to work—it's no big deal."

"Oh. Okay." I leaned against the window, feeling the cold outside through the glass. The only light was the quarter moon, and the trees looked like a black drape against the dark blue sky.

"Johnny, don't freak out. It's going to be fun. You've got the routine down, right?"

"I know the song by heart."

"Okay, then. Don't sweat it. You're gonna be great."

"It's not that . . . I mean, it is. But . . . I mean, is

it gonna be like . . . do you think they'll . . . do you think they'll be able to tell?"

"Tell what?"

"I mean, it's a gay bar. But I'm not really . . . you know. Gay."

"Johnny." She laughed. "You're *performing*. Gay or straight doesn't matter."

"I don't want them to think I'm being disrespectful or anything."

"You're putting on a dress and lip-synching to Blondie. Trust me, the gay community will recover."

"Maria." I laughed. "You know what I mean. I feel like everybody can tell."

"Tell what?"

"That I'm in love—" I stopped. Somehow I hadn't meant for the words to come out so quickly. Or at all. "With you."

"Oh." I could hear movement on the other end of the line. She was turning the stereo off. I wished she would say something. I wished she would laugh. I wished I had a rewind button on my mouth.

"I can tell, Johnny," she said, finally.

"Yeah?"

"Yeah. And I— Johnny?" There was a click on the line.

"Maria?"

"I gotta go. It's my dad trying to call in. I'll see you in school tomorrow, okay?"

"Okay."

There was another click, and she was gone.

My palms were sweating as we pulled into the parking lot of Club Mod. The place was packed, and it was only nine-thirty. I went ahead inside while Maria parked her father's rusty Ford pickup.

A drag queen in a tall pink beehive and a bouncer in black were manning the door. The thump of bass was coming from inside.

"ID, please," the drag queen asked. I brandished my fake ID. She looked at me suspiciously.

"I'm here to compete. For Night of a Thousand Divas." My voice squeaked. Be cool, Johnny.

"Okay, registration table's on the right of the bar. Just ask someone there to show you to the dressing rooms." She let me in with a wink. "Good luck!"

I ducked in and was immediately engulfed in

pounding bass. It seemed like everyone was bigger, older, and prettier than me. They were all men. And they were all staring.

I found the registration table, right next to the bar. I saw the bottles all lined up, tequila, vodka, gin, rum. *Stay focused. Think about Debbie.*

"Are you competing tonight?" A wiry guy dressed all in black asked me. I could only nod.

"Okay, just fill this out, give us your music, and the dressing room's right through that door next to the stage." I took a pen, scribbled in the blanks, and handed the form back to him, along with my copy of *Parallel Lines.*

"You're *Debbie*?" His eyes lit up when he saw the record.

"Yeah." I felt a little defensive. And a lot out of my element.

"I *love* her! I haven't seen a good Debbie in years! Can't wait!"

"Um, okay. Thanks."

He gave me a little wave as I headed back to the dressing room.

Inside, there was a long row of mirrors, a dressing screen, and an explosion of clothes and makeup.

The men—well, women—were frantically dressing, fixing their wigs, and applying makeup. I found an empty mirror and set down my bag.

"Watch out. That's Janet's seat." I looked over. The spitting image of Cher in the "If I Could Turn Back Time" video was speaking to me. I picked up my bag quickly.

"Janet?"

"Miss Jackson, if you're nasty." She motioned over her shoulder to someone who looked exactly like Janet Jackson. "She's the returning champion. Last year was the first time in five years anybody ever beat Tina there." She pointed down the row of mirrors to someone who looked exactly like Tina Turner.

"So Janet stole the crown from Tina, and now Tina wants it back?"

"You got it, babe." Cher blotted her lipstick. "But I'm almost done. You can have my spot."

"Thanks. I'm gonna . . . go get changed." I took my duffel and went behind the screen. My hands were trembling a little as I opened the bag and unrolled my dress. I'd folded it in the special camping way my dad showed me, so there were no wrinkles in it. I managed to get myself into Maria's bra, stuff it with socks, and pull my pantyhose on in record time. When I emerged, Cher saw me and gasped.

"Oh my God! What are those things?" She poked me in the socks.

"Hey!"

"Just as I suspected." She reached in and pulled out my left one. "What do you think this is, 1950? Ditch those. I've got just what you need." She retrieved what looked like a tackle box from under the counter. It was chock-full of makeup and hair clasps.

"Who are you supposed to be, anyway? Marilyn?"

"Debbie Harry. From Blondie."

"Oh, of course! I love her. These are perfect, then." She pulled out a plastic case about the same size as a jewelry box. When she opened it, there were two flesh-colored blobs inside that looked like raw chicken cutlets. With nipples.

"What the heck—"

"Just slide them in. They look so natural, you're not going to believe it." I took out the socks and tucked the rubber tits inside Maria's bra. Cher straightened them and turned me around so I could see my reflection.

"These are . . . frighteningly realistic," I murmured, giving the left one a poke.

"Welcome to the nineties, honey. I want them back after the show, though." She looked up at the clock on the wall. "Okay, I'm going out for a drink. See you at showtime!"

I sat down in her chair. I couldn't stop looking in the mirror. From the neck up, I was me. But from the neck down, I was . . . something else entirely.

"Johnny!" Maria burst in, holding my hair. "You forgot your wig—" She stopped short when she saw my cleavage. "Oh, my God."

The guy from the registration table poked his head in the door. "Okay, everybody, thirty minutes to curtain!"

"Thirty minutes, thank you!" A chorus of voices rang out, followed by squeals and frantic scurrying.

"That's plenty of time." Maria put her hand on my shoulder. I felt calm right away. She bent over and kissed me on the head, near my ear. "You're beautiful already," she whispered.

. . .

I was barefoot in the wings, holding my stilettos. Maria was next to me, gnawing on a fingernail. Janet was up, doing the routine from the "If" video. She had one of the bouncers dancing with her. It was mesmerizing.

"I don't know how they do it," Maria whispered.

"Do what?"

"Look so beautiful! It's unfair. Some of these guys are even prettier than real women!"

"It takes twice as much effort," I reassured her.

"There you are!" It was Cher. I had a sudden terrified thought that she wanted her breasts back. "I wanted to wish you luck—it's your first time, isn't it?" I nodded. "I thought so. I hope you don't think I'm being too presumptuous, but you kind of remind me of me when I first started."

"I'm flattered," I replied.

"So who's she supposed to be?" Cher nodded at Maria.

"His girlfriend," Maria told her firmly.

"You don't say. Well, my pleasure." Cher extended her hand, looking a little surprised. Maria shook hands and gave her a polite smile. Onstage, Janet's routine ended, and there was thunderous applause.

"Can you believe that's legal? Using another dancer?" Cher shook her head. "Oh my God!"

There was another Cher onstage. This one was wearing a huge feathered headdress and launching into "Half Breed."

"She's not that good," Maria tried to assure her.

"It doesn't matter." Our Cher sank dejectedly into a folding chair. "She's Bob Mackie Cher. I'm eighties, Bagel Boy Cher. And a Bob Mackie always beats a Bagel Boy. Every time."

"Well, maybe not this time." I tried to cheer her up. "Remember, last year Janet beat Tina. This may be your year for an upset."

"I don't know. How does she look out there? I can't watch." Our Cher swigged miserably from an Evian bottle.

"She's not a very good dancer." I peeked around the curtain. "And, um . . . I think her lip-synching is a little off."

"You're a doll," she told me.

"Johnny!" Maria hissed. "You're up next!" My

stomach tied itself into a quick knot and I slipped quickly into my stilettos.

"Break a heel!" Cher whispered.

"Thanks!" I wobbled over to the wings just as Bob Mackie Cher was giving her big finish. The announcer broke in on the applause.

"Next up, please welcome, all the way from New York City . . ."

"I'd kiss you, but I'd smear your lipstick," Maria whispered. I squeezed her hand. This was it. I silently prayed that the stilettos wouldn't fall apart mid-shimmy.

"Miss Deborah Harry of Blondie!"

The first few beats of "Heart of Glass" started. I couldn't move.

"Go be Debbie!" Maria gave me a little shove. Next thing I knew, I was standing out onstage. A blast of wild hoots and hollers shot up from the blurry darkness in front of me. It was like looking into an eclipse. A sudden thought ran through my mind of Janet, of Tina, of the two Chers. I was never going to win this. *What in the hell am I doing here?* Then, I thought about Maria, and her mom, and the seven hundred dollars.

"*Once I had a love!*" I crowed. But it wasn't me. The crowd was going crazy, but not for me. For Debbie. For Debbie's voice, Debbie's strut, Debbie's little white dress and bleach job.

And, maybe, just a little, they were cheering for me. Just for putting it all on.

The song whipped by in a blur. I don't know if I remembered my moves. I stopped being me, stopped thinking about Johnny in a Dress, and let the song carry me. I felt like I was carrying Debbie's voice, and the music was carrying me. I felt open, like a window, a conduit, all those things.

But I was never Debbie herself. I could almost imagine it. *It's 1978, it's CBGB, it's New York City, and I'm—*

Almost. But not quite.

The song ended. The crowd applauded. I did a little curtsey and made it backstage without tripping. Maria grabbed me and kissed me hard on the mouth.

"Johnny! Oh my gosh! That was insane!"

"Was I good? Was it okay?"

"Was it *okay*? Holy crap! Johnny, you had them eating out of your hand! It's like you were *her*!"

"Are you sure this is your first time?" Cher eyed me suspiciously.

"I—I—" I didn't know what to say. I felt like I had stood up too fast. There were still little spots swimming in front of my eyes from the lights. Maria just threw her arms around me and smashed her lips against mine. No need to worry about smudging the lipstick now.

Pretty Baby

The contest was over. Our Cher did a great rendition of "If I Could Turn Back Time," and Tina brought the house down. But we had to wait for the judges to make their decisions. Maria and Cher were dancing to eighties music with the pink-beehived door girl. I was watching them, sitting it out at the bar. My stilettos were killing me.

"Hey, Debbie." The bartender tapped me on the shoulder. He was holding a pinkish-colored drink. "This is for you."

"I didn't order it."

"It's from him." He motioned to an older guy at

the end of the bar with an earring and carefully cultivated beard stubble. If drag queens dressed as men, he could've been George Michael.

"That's nice, but I can't drink," I shouted over a Eurythmics remix.

"Listen"—the bartender motioned me closer—"you might want to take this. He runs the joint. And he has the final say in who wins the contest. Know what I mean?" I felt the tiny hairs on my neck prickle.

"Okay." I took the drink. "Thanks." It was cold in my hand. I took out the stirrer and licked it. Sex on the Beach. Subtle.

"Hi." Stubbly Guy walked up to me. "I really loved your performance. I'm a huge Blondie fan."

"Oh." I tried to smile. "Well, listen, thanks a lot, but I can't take this."

"What?" He leaned closer. His cologne was sharp in my nose.

"I—I can't take this drink. It's nothing personal, I'm just a—recovering alcoholic."

"Oh, I'm so sorry! Here, give me that." He took it out of my hand and took a sip before setting it back on the bar. "I'm Anthony."

"I'm . . . uh . . . Debbie."

"Oh my gosh!" He pulled his head back abruptly as a lone saxophone pierced the air. "It's Romeo Void! I love this song! Come dance with me!"

"I can't, my shoes—" But he was already pulling me out onto the dance floor. I looked around for Maria to rescue me. She was nowhere. Anthony started dancing about a foot away from me. I moved a little, my feet aching. It was only a second before Anthony's hands were around my waist, pulling me toward him. I could feel tiny beads of sweat poke out above my lip. *He knows I'm a guy, right?* My mind was racing. *Right?*

"I really loved your act." I could feel his stubble against my cheek again. His hands were slowly moving down my back.

And then I found Maria. Or, rather, she found me.

Time does strange things. Stretches, condenses. Seconds seem to take days. It only took a split second to see the look in her eyes. For Anthony to tighten his hands around my ass. For her to turn and leave. For me to push him away. It was only a second, maybe two. In real time. But this had stopped seeming real a long time ago.

"Maria!" I called out to her.

"Hey." He grabbed my arm. I'd nearly knocked him down. The people around us were staring.

"That's my girlfriend," I told him, wrenching out of his hand. I shoved my way through the guys in leather pants and the divas. I ran backstage. To the lounge upstairs. To the ladies' room, even. I finally found her outside, sitting on the hood of her truck.

"Maria." She didn't look at me. She'd either been crying or was about to start. "Listen, that guy owns the club. He bought me a drink. I turned it down, but then the bartender told me who he was and said that he was in charge of who wins the contest, so I tried to apologize for turning down the drink and he pulled me out on the dance floor and next thing I know his hands are all over my ass!" I was out of breath. And I felt suddenly ridiculous. I was conscious of my skinny arms sticking out of the dress and my crooked wig. Just looking at Maria, I felt like somebody was stabbing me in the heart. *I don't deserve her,* I thought.

"So you think he'll give you the grand prize, now that he's copped a good feel?" Maria said slowly.

"Considering I just about knocked him on his ass, I don't know if they're even going to let me back into the club." Maria kind of laughed and shook her head. She was so beautiful, sitting there on the hood.

"Johnny, it's a gay bar. A man asked you to dance. What did you expect?"

"I don't know." I was surprised. I honestly didn't know. "It wasn't me. I mean . . . I wasn't myself."

"Maybe you were yourself. Maybe I'm the one who's kidding myself."

"What do you mean?"

"What do I mean? Last night you said"—she rubbed her eyes. "Never mind. I shouldn't have brought you here, Johnny. I'm sorry."

"Hey, you two, they're announcing it!" It was our Cher, beckoning to us from across the parking lot.

"Come on." Maria got down off the truck.

"Wait a second. Are you mad at me?"

"I don't know. . . . I'm confused. Let's just go see who wins." She walked back inside, and I followed behind her.

Onstage, the MC was opening envelopes. Anthony stood to the side of the stage. We found a spot next to our Cher. The music went down.

"Third place and the two-hundred-dollar prize goes to Janet Jackson, 'If'!"

"Oh my gosh." Cher was stunned. Janet accepted her check with a huff.

"Second place and the four-hundred-dollar prize goes to Tina Turner, for her 'Proud Mary/ Nutbush City Limits' medley!"

"Tina got *second*?" Cher grabbed my arm. "Then first could be—*anybody*!"

"And now, the winner of the seven-hundred-dollar grand prize . . . Cher!" But which one? Cher's nails dug into my arm. "For 'If I Could Turn Back Time'!"

Our Cher was squealing and jumping up and down. Maria and I cheered. The crowd roared. And as she took the stage, I saw Anthony wink at our Cher. Our Cher gave him a little wave.

"Well, I guess that's it," Maria said.

"Yeah, let's split." We turned to work our way through the crowd.

"And our final award of the evening." The MC tried to regain control of the cheering crowd. "The Audience Award and seventy-five-dollar gift certificate to Manny's Leather World goes to . . . Debbie Harry, 'Heart of Glass'!"

I froze. The DJ started playing the song. Maria looked at me, stunned. I laughed once, like a hiccup.

"Well, go on!" she finally stammered. I sleep-walked toward the stage, a hundred faces mouthing "You go, girl!" at me. I glanced at Anthony. He was looking at his cuticles.

Just as I started to step up to the stage, a man's hand landed on my shoulder.

"Good show, John!"

I turned around. There, in all his grinning, bleached-blond glory, was Mr. Briggs.

Rapture

"What time is it?" I had fallen asleep.

"Almost four in the morning." Maria turned off the engine. I wiped drool off my hand and looked around. We were sitting in her driveway. She was still wearing her seat belt.

"So what's the deal?" Her voice was soft, but there was something defensive about her body. She seemed tensed. Like she was bracing for impact.

"What do you mean?" I knew what she meant.

"I mean with you and me. With you dancing with that guy. Did you really want to win all that much? Or is that just an excuse? I thought this was supposed to be *fun*. I thought I was helping you realize a dream or something, and now I feel like—I feel like you made a fool out of me tonight."

"Maria, I wanted to win for you!"

"For *me*? Slow dancing with some guy, how is that for me? Jesus, Johnny, I don't care if you're gay, or whatever, but you said—I mean, I thought you were—I thought you were *honest*."

"I am honest!" I interrupted. "Here!" I threw the gift certificate on the dashboard. "It was supposed to be seven hundred dollars so you could see your mom at Christmas! That was the only reason I wanted to do it in the first place."

Maria didn't say anything for a long time. The words I'd said just hung there, like a bell that wouldn't stop ringing. I stared straight ahead at the peeling trim on the garage, at the rusty basketball hoop, long netless.

"You were gonna give me the money?"

"Yeah." I bit my lip. "Fat lotta good a gift certificate does getting you to New York, huh?"

She smiled and shook her head. Her body relaxed.

"I don't care. That's the nicest thing anybody's

ever—" She stopped. Ran her finger along a crack in the dashboard.

I shrugged. "It *was* kinda fun up there, at least."

We both sat there in the dark. I knew I should go, but I didn't want to. I wanted to sit there next to her as long as she would have me. I had this feeling that once I stepped out of the car, she wouldn't talk to me again.

"Do you wanna come in?" she asked. I looked over at her.

"Do you want me to?"

"Johnny. Open the glove compartment," she commanded. I clicked the latch and the glove compartment door fell open. Sitting on top of the maps and the truck manual was a box of condoms. I felt a hot blush going all the way from my neck to the tops of my ears.

"Are those, uh—are those your dad's?"

"No!" Now she laughed. "They're mine. I mean, they're ours. If you want."

I unclicked my seat belt. Leaned forward and picked up the box. Thinking only, *Yeah. I want.*

I was more nervous than I was when I went onstage. We stood in front of each other in the near-dark of her room. I took her face in my hands and kissed her. She kissed me back, pulling me to her. Without walking, it seemed, we were in her bed, our fingers nipping at each other's buttons and zippers. And then we were in the middle of it, slipping into each other's bodies as gingerly and comfortably as slipping into a warm ocean.

It was nothing like it had been before, when I'd tried with other girls. None of the tripping, the fumbling, the uncomfortable shifting and apologies. Maybe it was because I was sober. Maybe because she was so sure of herself, and of me, too. All I knew was, when I was inside her, I felt relieved. Like I'd finally found where I belonged. And even after, when she was finally asleep, I stayed awake, watching her breathe, feeling the softness of her arms, memorizing the pink curls of her ears, smelling her scent and holding her so close that at times I could imagine that her body was my own.

I dreamed about Debbie again. This time, we were backstage at the Diva show. Wearing identical white dresses.

"I wanted to wish you luck," she said to me.

"Why?"

"You're going to need it." Somehow, it seemed foggy backstage and it was hard to see her. "I hope you don't think I'm being presumptuous, but you kind of remind me of me when I first started out."

"Well, I hope so," I told her. "That's kind of the point."

"Just remember"—she put both hands on my shoulders—"suspension of disbelief is a real thing. In fact, most people make it the number-one priority in their lives. Artifice is *the* most valuable human trait." I wasn't sure what she meant.

"I'm scared," I confessed.

"Don't worry, Johnny," she said, seeming even farther away. "She's going to love you. Everyone's going to love you." I tried to ask her another question, but somebody was already calling my name. Was it time to go on? I couldn't find my stilettos. Somebody called my name again. My eyes snapped open. It was Maria.

"Mmm—" I looked around. The room was pale gray with sunrise.

"Johnny, we better get up. My dad'll be home soon." Maria was sitting on the edge of the bed in her red satin kimono. I sat up and kissed her on the shoulder, like I'd wanted to that first night at her house. It already seemed like a thousand nights ago. Her skin was like milk. Maybe I was still dreaming.

"Are you okay?" I asked her.

"Yeah." She grinned and looked at me. "It's not like it was my first time, Johnny."

"Oh." I felt dumb. "It was mine."

"Oh." We were both quiet. "I mean, it's not like I had a lot of—I mean, there was only one other time," she tried to explain. "And it wasn't even—"

"Was it Brian?" I asked her suddenly.

"No. God, no. It was, um, someone in New York." She was blushing. "Are *you* okay?"

"Yeah. I'm great."

"I mean, are you okay with me? There's a lot of stuff I still haven't told you, Johnny, just about how I used to be, and stuff that happened in the city. . . . It's all kind of . . . kind of embarrassing."

"Losing your virginity isn't embarrassing. It's normal," I told her. "I don't think you're a slut or anything, if that's what you mean." I thought about what Lucas told me that day in the shop. I held her hand. "And, you know, everybody has problems, with their families, or—whatever. I have problems. It's okay."

"I know, but it's different, Johnny. I did some really stupid stuff. I used to— I didn't even feel angry or sad or anything. I didn't feel anything for so long. I just didn't want to exist." A tear spilled onto the blanket. I lifted her hand to my face and pushed up her kimono sleeve.

She was watching me, her eyes distorted behind tears that wouldn't fall. There were rows of tiny scars along the insides of her wrists. I kissed them and pressed my face against her skin. The tears finally rolled out of her eyes.

"Sometimes I feel like I'm the only person on the whole planet," she whispered.

"I know," I told her. I thought about my bare little room in Parkwood. About waking up at Terry's, trying to remember where I was. "I used to be all alone, too."

We held each other until her dad's friend dropped him off outside the house and I had to make a fast escape out the bathroom window.

I Know but I Don't Know

"Have a seat, John."

"Okay." I was back in Briggs's office on Monday. I sat down, feeling nervous. I crossed my legs. My toe bonk-bonk-bonked against the side of the desk. He crunched cashews and studied me, his pen tap-tap-tapping on his notebook. Together we made a fair rhythm section.

"Okay." He stopped tapping. "So, John, let's just get it out of the way. Start fresh, clean slate, and all that."

"All right." I sat up straight.

"Are you gay?"

"I don't think so," I answered. Thinking about Maria. Her milky skin.

"Because, John, if you are, I want you to feel like you have someone to talk to. You're obviously"—he shifted in his seat—"not alone."

"I know."

"It's just that these years can be hard for anyone, gay, straight, bisexual. Do you know how high the suicide rate is among gay teenagers?"

"No."

"It's high. Damn high. Because, so many times, kids of alternative sexualities don't feel they have anyone to turn to. Especially in small towns. They feel ashamed, afraid their parents will disapprove, afraid of what other kids will say and do. I don't want you to feel scared or ashamed, John." He was leaning forward in his seat, getting really into his speech.

"I don't feel that way," I tried to convince him. "Look, Mr. Briggs, I appreciate what you're trying to do. But I—" I took a deep breath and looked out the window. A bunch of kids were hanging out beneath the big tree in the courtyard, reading and joking.

"I don't know what to call it. I don't feel attracted to men." He was looking at me like he was waiting for something. "I know what kids say about me here. It pissed me off at first, but what can I do about it? I'm the new kid. New kids are supposed to get picked on. And I don't exactly give them any reason to think I'm *not* gay. I'm not interested in sports. I'm short. I dress funny. Heck, I barely have to shave."

He laughed. "You don't mind kids taunting you?"

"Of course I mind. But what can I do, go around punching everybody that calls me faggot? Flex my muscles and prove how manly I am? Forget it."

"You could report them."

"Come on." I looked at him. "They'll get a slap on the wrist for calling me queer and then they'll come kick my ass for ratting them out. Good plan."

"John—"

"Listen, sticks and stones, okay? It's not worth it. I mean, thanks anyway, but I can take care of myself."

"Okay, then." He was quiet again. "So, how about that dress?"

"How about it?" I was getting tired of all this.

"Are you a transvestite?"

"A what?"

"A transvestite. Someone who dresses in the clothes of the opposite gender. Do you wear women's dresses often?"

"Not *often.*" I shrugged. "I mean, sometimes I wore eyeliner and lipstick at the Goth clubs in Florida. But that was different. The dress is a more recent development."

He glanced at his notebook. "Is Deborah Harry one of the girls you think about to keep from drinking?"

"Yeah. It's not like I just think of Debbie and, bang, I'm cured. It's . . . I dunno, meditation or something. If I'm in a tough situation, I think about how cool and tough she is, and I try to be cool and tough, too."

"So by dressing up like her—"

"It's the first time I've ever done it. I'm still kind of trying to figure it out myself. It was fun."

Briggs was scratching away at his notebook. He looked up. "Fun?"

"Yeah. To get up there and be fabulous for a few minutes. To have everybody cheering me on. Even though it wasn't really *me* they were cheering . . . I kinda liked it."

"John, do you wish you were a girl?"

I had to think for a minute. Did I really want to *be* Debbie, or any woman? Did I want to be myself but with a different set of equipment? Was that the key? It seemed like a whole new set of problems.

"I like—I *love* women. They're beautiful and—they're just different. Sometimes I wish I could be gentle and beautiful and not be called a queer. But I don't hate myself or anything. I'm doing better, right? My grades are okay. I'm not getting into trouble. So what's wrong with putting on a dress every once in a while?"

"Nothing, John," Briggs said after a while. He put down his pen. "I'll see you next week."

Attack of the Giant Ants

I got out of Briggs's office just as the lunch bell rang and looked for Maria, but she wasn't out by the bleachers. Her scooter wasn't outside, either. I went to the pay phone and dialed her house. No answer. She didn't show up for History, but a lot of kids were skipping since we had a substitute. I wondered if she was sick, or mad at me. I wondered if she regretted having sex with me.

Later, during French, one of the secretaries knocked on the door. She spoke quietly with Mademoiselle Sheffield, both of them looking serious. I looked at Maria's empty seat, and a sudden jolt of worry shook me. My hands felt sweaty. My mind jumped back to seventh grade. The vice principal outside the door with my math teacher, both of them whispering and looking grimly at me, shaking their heads. Mademoiselle Sheffield called me over. I made myself walk.

"Is it about Maria?"

"Yes."

I felt nauseous. I was twelve all over again. *Your father's had an accident, John.* Our neighbor waiting in the office to take me home, where my mom was wailing so loud they had to put her on sleeping pills. *Oh, God, please, please let Maria be all right. I know I haven't prayed in a while, but I'm a kid and I don't know any better. Please, please . . .*

"Come with me," the secretary said. "Her father wants to see you." I obeyed. The halls seemed twice as long. The secretary's heels clicked in front of me, but it seemed like they were miles away. What did Maria's father want with me? Maybe he found out we had sex, and now he'd come for me. A crazy thought, but it took my mind off the possibility that something bad had happened to Maria.

A million years later, we got to the office. And

there was her father, standing in the lobby. He was huge. He looked like he should be carrying a metal lunchbox and welding something. He was dark-haired, like her, but it was hard to imagine him and Maria coexisting in the same house, let alone the same family. His eyes were red, but not with anger. He looked like he'd been up all night. Or, I guess, in his case, all day.

"You're Johnny?" he asked.

"Yeah. Yes, sir." My voice would barely come out.

"I'm Al Costello. Maria's dad." He extended his hand. It was like shaking a baseball mitt. "Maria's mother passed away yesterday," he blurted out. "Maria went to New York. To the funeral." I almost cried with relief.

"Oh!" I caught myself before I said *thank you, God,* out loud. Mr. Costello looked sad and faraway. "Oh," I said again, more softly. He just shrugged.

"She'll be back in a few days. But I thought you should know, since you're friends." He rubbed the back of his neck.

"Thanks—thank you, sir. Um, do you want me to pick up her assignments?"

"Oh, yeah, that's a good idea. I guess you can

just bring them by the house. You know where we live, right?" He squinted at me.

"Yeah. Yes. Sir. No problem. Is there anything—else I can do?"

He shrugged again. "I'm sure that when she gets back, she'll need somebody to talk to. So, you know. . . ."

"Of course." We were both just standing there. From a back room, we could hear a couple of secretaries laughing and the Xerox machine whirring away.

"Well, it's good to meet you, Johnny. Maria talks a lot about you." He gave me a sort of lopsided smile. Neither of us knew what else to say, so we shook hands again. I took a hall pass and went back to French.

The next day, we were dissecting frogs in Biology. Ben and I were paired up again. I took the scalpel without even asking and made the first incision.

"I heard about Maria's mom." Ben finally broke the silence. "Would you tell her I said I'm sorry?"

"Tell her yourself," I muttered, concentrating on the frog.

"Look, man, I don't know why Brian acts the way he does. You seem like an all right guy, even if you are gay."

I paused, tightening my grip on the scalpel. "I'm not gay," I said under my breath.

"Hey, whatever tickles your pickle, man. I don't pass judgment. But Maria and me used to hang out, so just tell her I said hey or something, okay?"

"Like I said, tell her yourself." I looked up at him.

Ben rubbed his eyes, trying hard not to look at any of the frogs in various states of dissection all around the room. The smell of formaldehyde was thick in the air.

"So, are you and her, you know—" He gave me a conspiratorial look.

"Are me and her what?"

"You know. I mean, if you're not gay—"

"None of your business." I held my head down, feeling myself blush.

"Aw, you're totally doin' it! I knew it!"

"Shh!" One of the kids from the table next to us was staring at me. "I don't kiss and tell."

"All right, I hear ya. You're a *gentleman*." He nudged me, and I nearly lopped off a frog leg.

"Hey, watch it. I wanna keep my thumbs."

"Sorry. Hey, seriously, though, if you want people to stop saying you're queer, you oughta, you know . . . let people know. That you're doin' it with her."

"Ben."

"Yeah, bro?"

"Stop saying 'doin' it,' willya?"

"I mean, she's no cheerleader or nothing, but you'd still be a playa."

"I don't care about that." I tried to change the subject. "Maybe we oughta just concentrate on the frog, huh?"

"I'm just saying." He shrugged. "I could help you out. If you want it to get around, you know."

"There's nothing about me and Maria that needs to get around this place." I had the frog's insides exposed. Splayed out like that, I felt a sudden pang of sympathy for the frog. I had this weird urge to cover it with a paper towel. Instead I just pushed the tray over toward Ben. "Now, you wanna take some notes on this frog's reproductive system, or what?"

"All right. Sure." He got out his pen and looked

over at my dissection. "Okay . . . that looks like the . . . uh . . . hang on." One look at the frog and Ben was up in a flash, bolting to the door again with his hand over his mouth. This time, Mrs. Van Horn, the teacher, was looking at me accusingly.

"Too much *Frogger* as a child," I explained. The kids next to me laughed. Mrs. Van Horn didn't. She gave me a pass to leave and make sure Ben was okay.

I went to the closest bathroom, but Ben wasn't there. I thought maybe he'd gone outside, so I walked down the hall and out to the bleachers, where a couple of the smokers were hanging out. Ben was there, pale and clammy-looking, but so were Brian and Donald. My stomach lurched. *What had Ben told them?*

"Hey, freak, who let you out of your cage?" Brian said.

"I just came to see about Ben. Mrs. Van Horn sent me." My voice nearly broke. I was nervous and trying to pretend I wasn't.

"I'm fine. Just too much formaldehyde or something. I'll come back," Ben said, wiping his forehead with the back of his hand. He still looked pretty dizzy.

"Aww, does the widdle girl have a widdle hall

pass?" Brian flicked his cigarette at me and grabbed the pass out of my hand.

"Knock it off, Brian." I grabbed it back. He swiped at me, and I ducked. "I'm serious—" I wished Maria was there. She would have put him down with just a look.

"Oh, he's *serious*." Brian made another grab for me and I jumped back. "Come here, you little—"

I knew I was about to get tackled. So I ran.

"Come back here, you chickenshit faggot," Brian hollered. I was pretty fast, though, and I ran as hard as I could back to the science wing, to the boys' bathroom. At the last second, though, I changed my mind and ran into the girls' instead. Safe.

I ducked into an empty stall, trying to catch my breath. The door burst open. I jumped. Brian and Donald kicked the stall doors open until they found me.

"Should've known you'd run into the girls' room. Best place to find a pussy." I tried to run around him, but he grabbed me and held me in a headlock.

"Fuck you! Let me go!"

"Such language! How unladylike!" Brian dragged me over to the row of sinks.

"What the hell is your problem?" I shouted, thinking somebody had to hear the commotion and come in and break this party up. Mrs. Van Horn would be looking for me. Ben would come running in. *Somebody!*

"You're my problem. I don't like faggots. Especially when they're turning my old girlfriends into fag hags." I could feel his hot breath on my forehead. My stomach churned. I looked up at him, but from where he was holding me, all I could see were nostrils. He looked like a giant pig.

I couldn't help it. I started to laugh.

I don't know why. The whole thing just seemed so ridiculous all of a sudden. I couldn't stop laughing.

"What the hell are you laughing at?" His face reddened and he looked even more like a pig. I was nearly doubled over. "What the HELL are you LAUGHING at, FAGGOT?" His jaw clenched.

"You!" I choked out. "You think I had to turn your girlfriend into a fag hag? Look at you two. How come I never see you apart?" I stopped laughing and cleared my throat. "I think you two are in lo—"

Brian grabbed me by the throat, and I felt my

entire body being lifted off the ground. It took only a second, and then I was rushing backward, into a crashing sound. The back of my head shattered the mirror, and the last thing I saw was the surprised expression on Brian's face before he dropped me and I hit the cold tile floor, face-first.

Die Young, Stay Pretty

"Does it hurt when I do this?" Bug tapped my knee.

"No."

"What about this?" She tapped my other knee.

"No."

"Does it hurt here?" She poked my arm. I laughed. She was gripping her rocket notebook, which had temporarily become her doctor notebook.

"Nope, doesn't hurt there, either."

"What about here?" She poked me again in the arm. I laughed again, which actually did hurt. "Stop laughing! This is serious! You may be paralyzed!"

Bug looked at me with a dire expression on her face. I looked over her shoulder at Sam, who was trying not to laugh, either. He was talking to a lawyer. My mother was there, too. She had just flown in from Florida. We'd barely had a chance to talk, but I remembered seeing her first when I woke up from my thug-induced slumber, and I thought I'd gone back in time somehow to that night before I got sent to Parkwood. Now she and Sam and the lawyer were all gathered in my hospital room, where I had a head full of stitches, an IV drip, and a neck brace that suffocated like a turtleneck from hell.

"Well . . . if I was paralyzed . . ." I raised one eyebrow, Mr. Spock–style, at Bug, who was kneeling next to me on the hospital bed. "Could I do . . . this?" I yanked her notebook away and held it high above her head. I was no match for Dr. Bug, though. She stood up on the bed and grabbed it back easily.

"You're a terrible patient." She gave me a disapproving look and sat back down. Uncle Sam came over and lifted her off the bed.

"Hop down, sweet pea," he said. "We've got to talk to Johnny for a second." Bug settled into the big chair across the room, scratching away in her notebook. Mom and the lawyer stood at the foot of the bed.

"Johnny, this is Mr. Ray—he's a lawyer." My mother presented him.

"I know." I'd only been in the hospital a day, and I was sick of being babied. I wondered if Ray was his first name or his last name.

"John, I've spoken with attorneys for the Quinn family and for Langley Prep. The school wants to avoid a PR disaster, so they're willing to work with us in terms of a settlement. As are the Quinns, who want their son to have a shot at a wrestling scholarship, which he'll have if he can just leave the school quietly. Your mother and I have negotiated figures, and I think we've agreed on something that will satisfy all involved parties. Unless you sincerely wish to press charges, which is a long, drawn-out process I would advise against. Especially since you're dating the defendant's ex-girlfriend."

"Wait a minute." My head was spinning.

"Johnny, they're willing to offer you money to leave them alone. Do you really want to have to go to court and go through all this in front of everybody, and you might not even win?" My mother looked at me anxiously. Win what? I didn't care—I just didn't want to get beat up anymore.

"Just say the word and we can get the ball rolling, Johnny," Ray the Lawyer said.

"Johnny, you have a visitor," one of the nurses interrupted. Thank goodness.

"Who is it?"

The nurse stepped aside, and there was Maria.

"Can I have a minute?" I looked up at my mother. She looked at Maria, then back at me.

"A minute." My mom seemed annoyed. I didn't care. They all filed out, except Maria. Her black jacket was wrapped tight around her, like it was suddenly two sizes too big.

"Hey," she said. She came over to the bed and sat down on the edge.

"Hi." I took her hand. "You're a sight for black eyes."

"Same to ya."

We sat there in silence for a few minutes, holding hands. She looked tired as hell. Her eyes were dark, and her hair was messier than usual. But she was beautiful.

"Maria, can I ask you a stupid question?"

"Sure."

"Did they shave off all my hair?"

"No." She rolled her eyes at me. "Well, let me see the back." I sat up woozily. She examined the back of my head.

"That's a lot of stitches. But your hair's just long enough to cover up the bald spot."

"That's good." I settled back down. "I'm starting to feel like a hockey player." She smiled and I squeezed her hand. "I'm sorry about your mom."

"Thanks." She bit her lip. "Well, I guess I finally made it to New York, after all. Bereavement fares, you know." She gave a halfhearted smile.

"Are you okay?"

"I'm dealing."

"Well, if you want to talk—"

"I know." She looked at me. "My mom was a drug addict, Johnny. I spent the whole time I lived with her finding all her little stashes and getting rid of them." Maria sighed and shook her head. "I never wanted to believe it, even when it was right in front of me. And now . . . it's like . . . I almost feel relieved. Before, I was always thinking about her, worrying about her, wondering if she was okay, and wishing I could be with her. Just to take care of her. And now at least . . . at least I know exactly where she is. It's like, now I can finally stop worrying. Is that totally messed up?"

"No. Only slightly," I whispered.

She laughed. "God, Johnny, I'm so sorry about this."

"Sorry about what? You're not the one who oughta apologize!"

"But I don't know how else to say it. I just feel so *sorry*. All these bad things are happening, and I don't want them to. I don't know how to stop it." She sounded like a little kid all of a sudden. I wished I was a cartoon, a big hulking thing that could stop a speeding train with one hand.

"You can't stop it. Bad things just happen. And then good things happen. Good things will happen again. I know it."

"The eternal optimist." She smirked at me.

"I've been called worse." I shrugged. We both sat there for a minute. It seemed like years had passed since I'd held her in her bed.

"All I know is," she said, "thank goodness for Ben."

"What?" My mind snapped back from her bed to the hospital room at breakneck speed. "Thank goodness for Ben? Gee, how romantic of you. It's half his fault I'm here."

"But he—" Maria gave me a confused look. "You don't know what happened after Brian jumped you in the bathroom?"

"No, but, please, I'm all ears."

"Ben's the one who found you. He got somebody to call 911, and he got Mrs. Van Horn to take care of you until the ambulance got to school. Then he went and found Brian and Donald and turned them in. Some people are saying if he hadn't found you when he did, you might not have . . . well . . ." She smiled a little, but I could tell she was about to cry.

"Hey, no bad thoughts allowed in here. You're gonna wreck my good vibe. I might relapse." I squeezed her hand.

She sniffled and rolled her eyes. "Oh, yeah? Would this relapse include red lipstick and an a capella rendition of 'Boys Don't Cry'?"

"Don't forget the black nail polish."

Maria laughed. "I can't wait until you go through a Bowie phase."

"Hang around, I probably will." I would've gone through any phase in the world just to hear her laugh again.

"You know everybody's calling it a gay bashing," Maria told me. "It's in the newspaper and everything."

"I know. My mom hired this sleazy lawyer, and he says if we go to trial we won't win since I'm dating you, but if we settle, we can get all this money from the school and Brian's family. My mom just got here, and all she can deal with is the money. She's barely even talked to me."

"Gross."

"I know."

"What's the matter with people?" Maria shook her head.

"They're all crazy."

"Everybody but us."

"Well, yeah. Of course. We're the only normal people here." I smiled at her. She smiled back, closing her eyes.

"You make me laugh, Johnny."

"It's the least I can do."

We held hands for a long time. Neither of us was laughing.

• • •

The next day, Mom and Uncle Sam took me home. I had to go out in a wheelchair, even though I could walk. I had to wear a neck brace, too, which I fully intended on ripping off as soon as we were out of the doctors' sight. There were all these reporters outside taking pictures and trying to get a quote as we dashed to the car. It was insane.

"John! Do you have a comment? On behalf of gay teens?" A bunch of microphones all poked into my face.

"Um, I'm actually . . . not gay." There was a weird rustle from the reporters, then a bunch of yelling.

"So you deny your homosexuality?" one of them called out.

"No, it's just—I have a girlfriend and every-thing, so—"

"What do you have to say to your attacker?" *Nothing you're allowed to say on TV,* I thought. "Well, I just hope he can learn to be cool, you know?"

"Okay, people, that's enough." Mom and two male nurses pushed me through to Uncle Sam's car.

"Any final words, John?" One of the reporters tried to follow us.

"Uh, just thanks to everybody who sent cards and flowers and stuff." *Bang!* The car door closed, and we drove away in silence.

"I want you to come back to Florida," Mom announced when we got back to Uncle Sam's. "This is a crazy place. I don't know what I was thinking."

"You were afraid I was turning into a drunk."

"Well, you were!"

"Yes, I was." I was calm. Bug was watching us from the kitchen.

"And now you're turning into a gay!"

"Come on." I rolled my eyes.

"Are you a gay, John?"

"Where are you going to send me if I am?"

"John." She held up her hands. Her skin was pale. Uncle Sam came in and handed her a glass of water.

"Theresa"—he spoke to her softly—"John's nearly a grown man. He hasn't given me any trouble, and since he's been here he's done nothing but try and make the best of an unfortunate situation. I don't think it's right to just keep jerking him around from place to place—"

"Sam, please."

"All right." He backed away. Uncle Sam walked into the kitchen and persuaded Bug to go outside with him. I found myself wishing he would stay. Mom took a sip of her water.

"Look, Mom, I'm not trying to be a jerk. I don't think I'm gay—I have a girlfriend here. But I—" I stopped. Well, something horrible was going to happen to me either way. Why not be honest? "I think I'm a transvestite."

"Oh, Jesus God!" My mother grabbed her temples like someone in a Tylenol commercial.

"Well, it could be a hell of a lot worse!"

"How?"

"I could be a thug who goes around beating the crap out of transvestites!" I sat down in Uncle Sam's leather chair. I wasn't going to win a screaming match. I clenched my teeth.

"A transvestite. I suppose now you'll want a sex change."

"No, that's transsexual. Transvestites just like wearing dresses." I'd been doing my research.

"Some relief." She threw up her hands. "What do

you think your father would say if he could see you right now?"

What would he say? I imagined him laughing at Mike Myers in his big glasses doing *Coffee Talk*. I imagined all three of us laughing at all this stuff.

"I don't know, Mom. It's just you and me here."

"You're coming back to Florida."

"No, I'm not."

"Yes, you are!"

"Mom!" I jumped back up. "Will you listen to me? Look at me! Look at *me*, Mom. What difference is it going to make where I am? I'm different! You can't just . . . smooth me out and make me a regular guy. I'm not like Dad." Her breath caught a little when I said it.

"Your father and I— It's none of your business!"

"It's every bit my business. I know how he was. Uncle Sam told me he was exotic and artistic and you made him settle down and get a job—"

"He wanted to! It was his decision!"

"And it's my decision to stay here!" I had to sit down again. My head hurt and my throat stung. "Mom, you did what you thought was right, sending me here. I was mad at you for a long time for doing it. But I'm trying to make the best of it. I actually kind of . . . I kind of like it here now, with Sam and Bug. Maria means a lot to me. And I want to make it through the year. After May, I'll think about coming back to Florida to graduate. Okay?"

She sat down. She seemed exhausted.

"I miss you, Mom."

"I miss you, too, Johnny."

"I don't want to take the money."

"What money?"

"The lawyer's money," I said. "Or the school's money. Whoever's. I don't like that guy."

"We don't have to do any of that," she said.

"You won't be mad?" I was surprised. It's not like we couldn't use it.

"It's your decision. I don't blame you for not wanting to get involved with some ambulance chaser." She shook her head and sighed. "Johnny, I've made a lot of mistakes, and I know it doesn't always seem like it, but I really do just want you to be happy."

"As long as I wear what you approve of and behave myself, right?"

"Here's the deal. You can wear whatever you want, as long as I don't have to rush to the hospital in the middle of the night to see you lying uncon-scious in an emergency room. Okay?"

Boy, now I felt like a jerk.

"Well, the second time wasn't my fault." I tried not to sound so sarcastic.

"I know, honey. I wish I could've protected you. I'm just so upset that I—"

"Mom. It's not your fault, either," I told her. She nodded. I was afraid she was about to cry. I kind of wanted to put my arm around her, but I didn't.

After a while, she leaned over and patted my knee.

"You really like this girl Maria?"

"Yeah." I didn't even have to think about it. All of this other stuff—the school, the uniform, the bul-lies, the boring town—I'd take it all just to be with her. "I love her."

Forgive and Forget

Bug peered out a curtain tear at the tinsel-draped auditorium of the James Boyd Elementary School. Maria and I were backstage, helping her into her costume.

"What if I forget my lines?" She had to say a little prepared speech about Sally Ride that Maria and I had been taking turns drilling her on for most of the afternoon.

"Just make something up. You know enough about space." I couldn't reassure her enough. I knew it was more than just stage fright, though. Her mom was here, too—there had already been an awkward run-in between her and Sam in the school hallway.

"What if nobody likes my costume?"

"They're gonna love this costume," Maria insisted. She'd sewed most of it herself. "Just be yourself, and it'll go fine."

"How am I supposed to be myself when I'm pretending to be somebody else?" Bug looked up at Maria. Maria looked over at me.

"Well, if you're being yourself, then . . . Well, I think what Maria means is if you get nervous or feel afraid, you just rely on the same things that Sally Ride would. Bravery. Intelligence. All the things in your speech."

As Bug mulled this over, she was approached by a tiny kid in a huge peacock-feathered cowboy hat, aviator shades, and fake mustache.

"Hey, Bug! Are you a spaceman?"

"Space*woman*, Jeremy," Bug informed him patiently. "I'm Sally Ride. What's your costume?"

"Richard Petty! Number 43!" The kid gave a huge grin.

"Hey, Johnny." I looked up—it was Ben. "What're you guys doing here?"

"This is my cousin Bug."

"Cool. Who're you, Sally Ride or something?"

Bug nodded, beaming.

"This is my brother Jeremy."

"Richard Petty!" Jeremy insisted.

"Sorry, man."

"Kids! I need everybody lining up over here!" A teacher was clapping her hands. Bug grabbed the motorcycle helmet Maria and I had bought for her at Goodwill and painted with the NASA logo.

"Break a leg, kiddo," I told her. She gave me the thumbs-up and took her place in line between Jeremy and a kid in a Michael Jordan jersey.

"Man, this stuff kills me." Ben laughed. The lights flicked on and off, and the crowd hushed. From the front, the music teacher played a medley of "America the Beautiful" and "It's Beginning to Look a Lot Like Christmas."

"Hey, you guys wanna go out for a smoke?" Ben suggested.

"Thought you'd never ask." Maria found a side door, and we all stepped out into a courtyard. They both lit up. I stuck my hands in my pockets and tried not to freeze.

"Haven't seen you around much, man," Ben said. It'd been a while since we'd dissected anything in Biology. "Got kinda crazy there for a while."

"Yeah. Tell me about it."

The reporters had hung around for a day or two, trying to uncover some new dirt, but there wasn't much more to tell. I became a lot less interesting when I wasn't lying in a hospital bed, and the gay-bashing angle seemed to fade once they realized that Brian was jealous over Maria. Most kids still gave me weird looks, but some of them joked with me about the reporters or came up and told me how much they hated Brian. One freshman even told me he was gay and afraid his dad was going to throw him out of the house. I got him an appointment with Mr. Briggs.

Inside, the auditorium burst into applause.

"Sounds like it's starting." Maria dropped her cigarette and crunched it. "I'm gonna go find us some seats."

She went inside and Ben and I stood there, listening to the kids warble Christmas carols.

"I've been meaning to say thanks," I blurted out. "For what you did. Turning Brian in. I know it must've been hard. He was your friend."

"Yeah. He was." Ben shrugged. "Didn't make it right, though. What he did." He took a drag on his cigarette, then flicked it on the sidewalk. "Let's go back in, man. I'm freezin' my boys off out here."

We went back inside, where a chorus line of Founding Fathers, NASCAR drivers, basketball players, and one spacewoman were singing "Feliz Navidad."

"I got an A plus!" Bug was jumping around the parking lot. "A plus on presentation and A plus on costume!"

"And there were two Betsy Rosses," Judy said. "It's a good thing you switched."

"And three Dale Earnhardts! But I was the only Sally Ride!"

"The only and the best," I assured her. Bug squeezed between Maria and me—we were holding hands.

"Thanks for helping me with the costume." Bug undid our hands and stuck herself between us. I counted to three, and Maria and I hoisted Bug a few inches off the ground. "I'm glad you moved here, Johnny."

"Me too." I counted to three, and this time Bug

leapt with us. In the dark, Uncle Sam reached over and ruffled my hair.

Suddenly we were all blinded by a huge black Range Rover that pulled right up in front of us with the brights on. A woman got out of the car. She wore leather boots with high heels and a huge scarf swept dramatically over one shoulder.

"Ruth! Come on, honey!" It took me a minute to remember who Ruth was. Bug. Only her mother called her Ruth.

"I forgot. I have to go to my mom's." Bug didn't let go of my hand.

"Hi, Connie," Sam said.

"Hi, Sam." I don't think my ex-aunt recognized me. And I was kind of glad.

"I don't wanna go," Bug whispered to me.

I knelt down to whisper in her ear. "I know. But what do you think Sally Ride would do?"

Bug finally dropped my hand. She hugged Sam and walked into the car lights, her helmet tucked tight under her arm.

I went to Rocksteady one day before the school holidays to finish my Christmas shopping. I hadn't seen Lucas in a while. Not since the whole Brian incident. I don't know why, but I felt embarrassed for Lucas to know about it.

"Lionel Richie?" I put the records I'd picked out on the counter. Lucas peered down his nose at me. "Linda Ronstadt? You goin' Lite FM on me now?"

"They're for my mom," I explained.

"Ah, good choice, then." He rang it up. "So, you been all right?"

"Yeah." I fumbled in my pocket for the cash. "I guess you heard about the whole thing. At my school."

"Yeah, I heard about it. How come you didn't tell me none of that?"

"I'm tellin' you now."

"I mean beforehand. We're friends, right?"

"Yeah." I only secretly thought of Lucas as my friend. And I figured it only went one way. He was a cool, older guy. I couldn't imagine he counted me among his list of friends.

"Damn straight we're friends," Lucas said. "I know where you're at, man. When I was in school, many, many years ago, I was the only black guy into punk rock. All my friends had Afros, and I had a

Mohawk. I got the piss taken out of me every day. Ran away three times, but I finally graduated. And the great thing is, once you get out in the real world, nobody cares anymore. As long as you pay the rent."

"I don't want to think about the real world," I said.

"It's not so bad." He held up his finger like an exclamation point, suddenly remembering something. "I almost forgot. I got a Christmas present for you." He reached under the counter and pulled out a CD in a plain white cardboard slipcover.

"What is it?"

"The new Blondie single."

"But the new album's not coming out till January!" I'd read it in one of Maria's *Mojo* magazines. For the first time since the early eighties, Blondie was getting back together and putting out a new album.

"It's a promo. Top secret. Merry Christmas."

I looked at the plain package. New Blondie. My fingers prickled. I pulled the CD out of the package and looked at the typed letters on the label.

Maria. The name of the song was "Maria."

Platinum Blonde

The new Blondie song was so great it inspired me to make a mix tape for Maria for Christmas. One entirely made up of songs with "Maria" in the title or the lyrics. Lucas helped me track down some obscure ones. I was rigging up a second tape deck when Uncle Sam knocked on my door.

"Busy, John?" He was holding a flashlight.

"Not really." I stood up.

"I wanted to give you your Christmas present." I was leaving that weekend to spend the holidays with my mom in Florida.

"You didn't have to get me anything," I told him,

following him down the hallway. He pulled the attic door down, unfolded the ladder, and started climbing up.

"Wait just a second and I'll turn the light on." I could hear him thumping around. He flipped a switch and the attic was illuminated. I climbed up. Sam was standing next to a box full of records and a steamer trunk.

"These things were your dad's when we were younger. I thought that, what with all your— Well, I thought you should have them." He shoved his hands in his pockets. I knelt down in front of the box. My dad's records. I thought he didn't even like music. The only things he'd left behind at our house were too-big sportcoats, paperwork, and a box full of greasy tools. What kind of records did he listen to as a kid? The Beatles? Frank Sinatra? Show tunes? I was prepared for anything.

I flipped through the box. The records were dusty and old-smelling. And carefully organized in alphabetical order, like one of the bins at Rocksteady. David Bowie. Mott the Hoople. Suzi Quatro. T. Rex. Slade.

My dad was a glam rocker.

I opened the steamer trunk. Inside, it smelled of cedar. It was full of clothes and shoes—sparkly tops, spandex pants, stack-heel boots. I pulled them all out, one by one. There were loose tubes of lipstick and eye makeup rolling around in the bottom. And a picture album. I opened it up.

"That's us right after he got back, around '74 or '75, I think," Uncle Sam said, standing over me. "I'm the one on the left." In the picture, Sam was wearing bell-bottom jeans and a denim work shirt. He was a foot taller and had a full beard. The guy on the right in the brocade waistcoat with the bleached blond hair was my dad.

"He went to England after high school," Sam told me. "He got a college scholarship there so he wouldn't have to go to Vietnam. When he finally came back, he had all this." Sam smiled. "Of course, our folks weren't having any of it. So he put it all away. He moved away and married your mom, and I kept all of it. But he never asked for it back." Uncle Sam put the flashlight down next to me. "Anyway, it's yours now. You really—" Sam was having a hard time keeping his voice even. "You remind me so much of him. He'd be proud of you, John."

I didn't know what to say. I got up and hugged my uncle Sam.

"Thank you."

Sam patted my head. "Merry Christmas, John." We both stepped away from each other. "I guess I'll let you have a minute."

I sat back down, staring at the pile of clothes. I listened as Sam descended the ladder and went off down the hall. There was a whoosh in the ducts as the heat came on. I flipped through the photo album. It was full of pictures of my dad in London. Not only did he have all his hair, it was long and dyed platinum blond. He always appeared with various configurations of the same five or six people. A few of them, I wasn't sure which were women and which were men.

I lugged the trunk and the records down to my room. I turned off all the lights except for my bedside lamp and picked a record out of the stack without looking. I put it on the turntable. As I opened the steamer trunk again, I had the strange feeling that my father was buried inside. That he had been there for years. I took off my clothes. I slid into his satin pants. His candy-striped top hugged my shoulders. I clipped on his big red costume earrings, and tottered on the high heels of his boots. I felt the bottom of the trunk for one of the lipstick tubes. It smelled and tasted horrible, like something left to rust under a rock. But I rolled it over my lips all the same.

When I was finished, I looked in the mirror.

"Hi, Dad," I said.

Call Me

"I wish you weren't going," Maria said. We were standing on the front lawn. Sam and Bug were waiting to drive me to the train.

"I'll be back. It's just Christmas break."

"I know. I just have this weird feeling that you're going to have a good time with all your old friends and you'll decide to stay."

"I promise I'll have a really lousy time." I tried to pull us out of the mushiness. I was going to miss her, too, but I didn't want to embarrass myself and get all choked up. It was already weird and sentimental, with her mom gone and everything. Neither one of us mentioned it, but I knew that's what she was thinking about.

"Johnny!" Bug yelled across the lawn. "You're gonna miss the train!"

"I'm coming!" I yelled back. I gave Maria the tape. She handed me a shoebox, taped shut, with a bow stuck on top.

"Thanks. This is yours—sorry about the wrapping."

"It's okay. Nothing says Christmas like shoes."

She smiled and hugged me. "Merry Christmas, Johnny."

"Merry Christmas." I held on to her for a minute, not feeling any cold. Then she pulled away, looking over at Uncle Sam and Bug watching us from the car. She landed a chaste kiss on my cheek. That would never do. I pulled her close to me and kissed her on the lips until Uncle Sam blew the car horn.

"Okay. I gotta go," I told her finally.

"Call me," she said, and hopped on her scooter. I walked to the car with the shoebox under my arm as she buzzed away.

"All right. I'm ready." I got in the back. Uncle Sam put the car in reverse.

I liked the train, the way the world moved along through the window, the way you could be still and moving at the same time. I decided I liked traveling. It was a good time to just sit and think. I thought about my dad, always on the road. I wondered how much he thought about the parts of him he left behind. I wondered if he missed that trunk, all his old records, his pictures, his strange friends, his clothes. Maybe he really did change, inside and out, into the dad I knew. The one who was quiet in the dark, whose radio only argued sports and politics.

I waited until we were out of town, speeding through farmland, to open Maria's gift. There was no way I could wait until Christmas. The tape came off with a pop. There was a note:

Johnny,
Got these from Mom's friend Lee in New York. He assured me that they once belonged

to the female lead singer of a certain local band who comes in to get her hair bleached every so often. Hope they fit.

Love,

M.

I pulled back the tissue paper. Inside was a pair of slightly worn, backless white high heels. They were decorated with tiny rhinestones. I looked around. Nobody was watching. And I didn't care if they were.

I untied my shoes to try them on.

Acknowledgments

Special thanks to Noel Kirby Smith, who gave this assignment in the first place; to Jeff Bens, whose persistence is epic; and to Emily Sylvan Kim and Kate Farrell, for getting it. Thank you to the North Carolina School of the Arts and to the Spartanburg Day School—*finis coronat opus.* Further gratitude to those who encouraged the writing from the ground up: Billie Lathan, Joe Koon, Dr. Barbara Cobb, Dr. Betsy DeCourcy-Wernette, and Laura Hart McKinny. Thank you, Elizabeth Eslami, for everything, and Ryan Thorpe, for everything else. Extra glitter on the thanks to Weegee Sanders and all the Odyssey kids. Thanks to Scott Lazar and to the Cornelia Street poets, especially Jackie Sheeler, Miriam Stanley, Bob Hart, Frank Simone, Maggie Balistreri, and John Proctor, for your support and for making New York City feel like home. Thanks to Sean Solowiej for your friendship, invaluable conversations, and motorcycle rides. Thanks, Mike and Wendy Fornatale, for showing up. Thank you to all of the artists mentioned in this book (and many who aren't) for all the verses, riffs, fashion sense, and menacing poses struck on stages and album covers alike that helped me and many other gawky kids in the far reaches of suburbia survive our hapless solitary teenagedoms. Thanks to my family in the Carolinas and Alabama for their love and good humor, and thank you to Manya, my first storyteller. Mucho big love to my mom, who taught me to read. And final thanks and appreciation to my great-uncle George, who always gave me books, and who should have lived to read this one.